BOUDICCA JONES AND THE QUIET REVOLUTION

Rebecca Ward

Cover design by: Anne Heasell

For our mothers: near, far, lost, loved.

CONTENTS

Each beat of her heart pounds through her head like a dead fish hitting the slab. As she turns to look at the house, a chill wind streams across her bruised eye making her wince.

The vast, old villa has definitely known better days. What is left of the late afternoon sun picks out a camouflage of peeling paint and green moss. Raggedy plants grow high out of broken iron guttering, waving an unruly welcome. Gaps beneath the steps to the front door reveal an uninviting gloom and a dank stench, and worn wooden boards barricade the front door and windows. Not altogether inviting.

With no doorbell or knocker, she picks up a small stone and throws it at the tiniest slither of blue window left in the fanlight. The sharp crack that follows goes right through her and as she turns to run when a huge 'WHAT?!' bellows out of the letterbox.

Tentatively, she looks back to the house and gaining her composure she approaches the door.

'WHAT?!' Spittle sprays right in her face.

'Hi. Sam? Samuel McCabe?' She surprises herself with the timidity of her voice. No reply. 'I'm Ruby Jones' daughter,' she whispers, already regretting coming to this house. 'Jones. My mother is Ruby. You know her from, well, *you know*...Do you think I might come in?' She waits, peering through the letterbox, but can't make out even an inch of who is behind it. She tries again, 'Ruby. Ruby Jones?'

'Yes, I heard you.' He speaks a little gentler. 'Go down the side passage.' A dirty nail leads a stubby finger out through the letterbox, points left and then disappears, slamming it shut.

She pushes aside some overgrown weeds and edges along a dark passageway littered with old boxes, muddy glass bottles and piles of newspapers. She is glad it is daytime; at night the creepiness factor would be off the scale. There is a wooden gate at the end. She knocks. Nothing. She twiddles the latch but it doesn't budge. She tries to work out a quick escape route. Can she get over the fence if she has to? There is a fine net fixed to the top of it. The gate looks rickety; perhaps she could kick it in? She is big on exit strategies, even before she's arrived.

'What on earth is this place…?' she thinks, trying to quash thoughts of serial killers and chain clanking dungeons. She places her right hand flat on her stomach. It is something her mum got her to do to calm her down when she got wound up as a kid. 'And breathe, just breathe,' she chants. She feels the rise and fall of her stomach but her meditative calm is short-lived. Her new 'friend' is back.

'HAIR!' he barks from the shadows, unbolting the gate.

'What?' she says, confused. 'What has hair got to do with anything?'

'Hair. Show me your hair!' he says impatiently.

She takes off her hat and unpins her plaits. Her russet locks tumble round her shoulders, she forces a smile like a beauty pageant contestant who will stop at nothing to win the crown. Except this beauty queen has a thumping black eye.

The gate swings open. Before her stands a grizzly bear of a man. Round-shouldered and pot-bellied, his face covered in bristles, a full head of silver-streaked hair, his swollen and worn hands clasped in front of him. A plaid shirt and jeans give him a younger look than his years, which she guesses is around 60. Hairy toes poke out of worn flip flops. She looks him square in the face, a smile twitches at the edge of his mouth and his fuzzy eyebrows raise in amusement. His eyes belie his age, active and sparkling. His whole life is there in his eyes and he has had *fun*.

'I know, gorgeous, right?!' he says cheekily, and gives a huge belly laugh. 'Get your arse in here girl. You never know who's lurking.' He grabs her arm and pulls her through, slamming the gate behind her.

She follows Sam into the most extraordinary garden she has ever seen. Huge oak trees hold up fine nets 30 feet above their heads, like a giant's strawberry patch. All at once there are flashes of vivid red, green and electric blue. Then yellow, white and the palest pink. As her eyes focus she sees more than a dozen parrots and parakeets perched high in the trees. As one they squawk and ca-caw a welcome serenade. The delight of this extraordinary kaleidoscope of feathery fireworks makes her convulse into giggles.

'Shut it!' Sam bellows. They screech even louder. 'That never works.' And he is laughing again, his shoulders bobbing up and down.

She follows him into the back of the house, sensing eyes on her but not sure where from. She has to get back on her guard. It had fallen in an instant, as Sam is so immediately likeable. Her mum would say he has a "good aura", but then again she knows that, he was her friend.

He leads her through a micro-jungle of potted plants to a small kitchen, piled high with dirty dishes. She follows Sam's particular route as he swerves round his own junk. She is glad to move quickly through the kitchen, it smells pretty rancid. Each plate a petri dish for some colonising organism. Through another door they emerge into a battered library of sorts. Makeshift shelves of breezeblocks and old pallets house hundreds of books, some so well-thumbed that their spines no longer reveal their contents. There are no windows in the room, just books from floor to ceiling. Two battered, brown leather armchairs sit like tired, old sows, content in the amber glow of a brass reading lamp. She inhales the powdery smell: like old hay tinged with vanilla. Some might find it suffocating. She finds it heavenly.

'Reed!' Sam calls out.

'For a man trying to keep a low profile he sure likes to shout,' she thinks.

She reaches out to take the nearest book but Sam shoots her a damning look. She retracts her hand, a moment away from whistling to look otherwise occupied.

'Reed!' he bawls once more, absentmindedly flicking through the book on the top of the nearest pile, which she makes out to be some kind of plumbing manual.

A tall, skinny boy slouches into the doorway, his thick black hair hanging across his eyes. She notices he is wearing black from head to toe, just like her. His knees have done their worst on his tight jeans, splitting them right across. A leather thong necklace buries its silver treasure under the collar of his faded shirt. He has no socks under his scuffed black trainers, his toes wiggle as she watches. The only part of him not slouching. She thinks he is probably just a year or so older than her, around seventeen but it is hard to tell without seeing his face. He takes a deep, pained breath and then says slowly and very calmly, 'You don't have to shout Sam. I am right here.' He continues to look at the floor without saying hello to her or even looking her way. 'Do you want some tea?' Sam says. Her eyes are transfixed on the boy's hands, covered in a myriad of silver skull rings. Nails bitten to stumps. 'Tea dear?' he repeats. It takes her a second to realise Sam is talking to her.

'Sure. I mean, yes. Thank you,' she mumbles, distracted by this boy who does not seem at all put out by having a stranger in their house.

Then her stomach rumbles loudly alerting the whole room to the fact that she hasn't eaten for hours. Sam chortles, 'And toast, definitely toast.' She is horrified, but Reed slinks out without a second glance.

Sam turns to her and smiles wearily. 'My nephew Reed,' he explains. 'Very serious young man, but very special.'

'Oh, right...' she says, thinking he seems pretty rude. But what does she know; she doesn't have a wealth of experience to draw from. Her knowledge of boys her age mostly comes from the books she reads – Heathcliff, Harry, Pip. Not your average boy on the street stuff. Maybe this is quite normal? Sam gestures for her to sit in one of the armchairs and she falls happily into it, relieved to be off her aching feet.

'My dear,' Sam begins, lowering himself into the other chair. 'I think it would not be entirely presumptuous of me to guess all is not well...Ruby. Did they get to her?'

She nods.

'Not good. Not good at all. I'll get onto the others. Those TrueSec imbeciles?'

She nods again feeling tears starting to well up and looks up to the ceiling to try to force them back down. She read that somewhere, though it doesn't seem to work in practice. If the tears are coming you can't force them back in using gravity. She rubs her sleeve across her eyes and Sam reaches across and pats her other arm.

'When did they come?' he asks, kindly.

'Erm last night, around six-ish,' she says, her voice catching. She just about gets that out without breaking down.

'You're safe now,' he says, allaying her primary fear, though of course that is just the tip of the iceberg.

Sam leaves her to go into the kitchen. She just stares unblinkingly around her. The room feels so permanent, established, and sturdy. Something she has never experienced before. But then she remembers the backyard aviary. It is definitely not your average household. Heavy with stress and tiredness her eyes close, her body needing to shut down. The kitchen clock tick ticks away next door, marking every single second of her solitude.

Panic rouses her from her deep sleep. She has been covered over with a huge, mothballed, fur coat. It is warm but she doesn't want to think what else might be living in it so she shrugs it off with a shiver and it scrunches up at her feet. A small amount of light picks out Reed's silhouette, he is stood leaning on the doorjamb again, watching her.

'Boudicca' he says, quietly and considered, like her name is a beautiful foreign word or a far-off star he is wishing on.

Before she can reply he turns on his heels, shutting the door between them.

'Bodi,' she calls out after him, but he is gone.

* * *

On Sundays Bodi's mum lets her wear whatever she wants from their stash of clothes. 'It is the day for individuality' her mum says. 'A way to give thanks for your freedom and the power of your mind to do what it likes.' Her mum is prone to grandiose statements, but today Bodi embraces the small amount of freedom that is hers.

She is wearing a red wool coat with a mottled ermine collar. Skinny blue jeans with paisley patches and a snakeskin belt. A vest top with a Smiley on it. Heavy army boots and stars on her socks. Her leather satchel jangles with badges, ribbons and charms. Her curly, long, red hair trails down her back. She is a sight to behold and though some may not consider it so, this is to her mind her Sunday Best.

Bodi has escaped home for the day. She is sick of being cooped up in the flat, so she is dawdling in Green Park enjoying the autumn sunshine on her face and ignoring the funny looks. The city gardeners have been busy pruning the beds and all is neat and chaste. Not a shrub out of place. Unusually for Bodi, the order aggravates her. She finds herself scouring the beds, seeking out any resilient weed that has survived the cull.

Someone standing right in her way brings her to a sudden stop, interrupting her daydreaming. She can't make out their face as the low-hanging sun blinds her, radiating around their silhouette like an Hallelujah! moment. They both do a polite side-step waltz, matching each other as they move. 'Sorry' they both mumble, stepping again, disentangling their shadows, and going their separate ways.

'The autumn sun's not going away without a fight,' thinks Bodi, soaking in the warmth on her face knowing the brittle change to winter is just days away. She meanders along the path, falling back into the carefree world of her own making. The park is heavenly quiet save for the thrum of the traffic and the gleeful squeal of an escaped toddler bounding across the grass.

The heart of the city is kept pristine for the country's President who comes and goes from her London residence in armoured cars, windows blacked out. Bodi presumes that they are blacked out on the inside as well, so little is her public compassion. She travels by car from one grand residence to another never setting foot outside her electric gates, dictating laws through a series of chinless lackeys. It has been years since anyone has seen her in the flesh. Myths abound that Populus, the city's army of dissidents, burned her face off before they disbanded; that her left hand has been replaced by a hook; that she killed her own family unflinchingly. There is a new myth every year. Everything is inflated and nothing substantiated, but it keeps civic contempt flowing like wine at a wake.

Giving in to the evening chill, Bodi gives up on her walk and heads home. A few streets over, she passes a truck which has backed into a telephone pole and wires are cascading down into the street. No one is helping the truck driver who is looking forlornly at his dented truck while batting off insults from disgruntled residents and shop owners. If he leaves the truck to get help he can't be sure it will be in one piece when he gets back. The wires may not get fixed for months, and the locals are starting to get angry with the driver. Before long he will have to risk leaving to find a nearby garage, which will no doubt charge him every penny he has to move his truck.

Here, less than a mile away from the park, it is like stepping back in time to The Blitz. Londoners live in decrepit buildings, alongside those that have disintegrated entirely. The power and water supply is hit and miss and people rely on ill-maintained telephone lines. Entire streets are closed off for being unsafe, where potholes have become craters and houses have crumbled into the gutter. Most families live in precarious structures, held up by blind faith.

The sun had shone brightly on the park and those few with the time and money to rest on a sunny Sunday afternoon, but beyond that the majority of lives are darker and lived on a shoestring. The middle class has dissolved like an aspirin to ease the President's biggest headache - accountability.

Bodi has never known the city any different. She has not lived in a thriving metropolis with tourists coursing in and out of its veins vibing off the 'buzz'. Her London is a carcass of its once vital self.

As Bodi makes her way home, she walks past sun-faded hoardings for luxury apartments advertising shiny, new lives. Behind them stand tall, empty shells: grey, windowless and uninhabitable. "Buy today in this exclusive development" is printed across photos of a glamorous couple whose smiling mouths have long since been scratched out. Next to them, a restaurant serves dirt black coffee from its side door and a corner shop is piled high with tins and packets of non-perishable goods. You eat what you can when you can and many go hungry. Bodi's stomach grumbles in recognition of that sad fact.

Realising the time, Bodi crosses the bridge to get home, the wind blowing off the river puts her on edge. She used to love crossing the river and revelling in its skyline, especially when the sun is setting so beautifully. It is the perfect way to appreciate the magnificence of the city without troubling yourself with its grimy reality. That all changed last year. She resists looking over the railing in case she sees another body lying in the mud below. At first she couldn't make out what it was: dumped furniture, a poor, abandoned dog…But no. The image of the bloated, grey figure washed up at low tide still haunts her. It makes Bodi pick up the pace and hurry back.

Nearing home, she does her coat up to the neck, ties her hair back hastily and pulls on a black beanie. This is not an area to stand out. Her right hand habitually holds firmly onto the strap of her satchel. Local kids often race past on stolen bikes and grab what they can. She once saw a pensioner knocked unconscious for a bag of tin cans.

Head down, gone is the showy confidence of earlier and a knot of fear starts to grow in her stomach. Across the street a squadron of junkies trip along on their toes racing towards their next high. Mums shriek for their kids to come indoors, NOW. Fierce, salivating dogs yank against their heavy chains pegged into front yards. Where Bodi lives is a ghetto, but it is the perfect place to disappear.

Nearly every new family who moves into her block of flats is concealing something or is on the run. Everyone assumes you have something to hide and consequently there is an unspoken honour code between this band of strangers. You don't ask questions.

The block's lights are just coming on, flickering blue-white neon tubes stripped of their casements. The harsh glare reveals the filth that covers the concrete blocks that were cobbled together for temporary housing more than four decades ago. Damp, grey washing hangs like shrouds across balconies, covering the skeletons of broken furniture, useless TVs, rusting bike wheels. Each flat the same: run down, cold, miserable, and each holds a different story of loss, wrongdoing and fear.

As Bodi rounds the corner to her block she stops dead in her tracks. A black van is parked just below the stairs to her flat. The paintwork is dull and rusty; it has blacked out windows and no other markings. She is instantly petrified. *They* are here. She has run through this day with her mum every week of her life, but now it is here she is unable to recall a single detail of what they had discussed. She feels sick to her stomach and her knees buckle. She falls against the wall. Her sight blurs, panic flooding through her. Stern voices echo from her flat but she can't hear what they are saying. She just recognises her mum's name being shouted repeatedly. Ruby.

Bodi stifles her first instinct, to rush to her mum's side. She makes for the van instead. Crouching low, she skitters to the side furthest from the flat, hoping she won't be seen. A rough cough from the other side of the vehicle makes her jump. She hears the sharp click and blow of a cigarette lighter igniting, the flame illuminating that side of the van for a few seconds. Shiny black military boots and a grey wool hat is all Bodi can see but she can put together the rest of the picture. Sallow, pockmarked face, sunglasses day or night, moustache, cropped hair, grey flannel army trousers, grey bomber jacket. It is TrueSec's Special Intelligence Command Unit. A true misnomer, there is little special or intelligent about them. On the street they are known simply as the S. I. C. or Sick Boys.

She waits, crouching, holding her breath, until he wanders off again. Thankfully he seems to have little patience. All the while commands and jeers from upstairs are being met with silence. Her mum has shut down.

Bodi looks around her, working out where she can hide. She sees the door to the building's rubbish room is open and she edges towards it. The wooden doors have slats, some are broken and she will just about be able to see what is going on. Inside the room grimy signs about tidiness and cleanliness are fervently ignored. The residents are meant to drop the garbage in large metal containers but most simply opened the door and throw their bag in, no matter what it contains. The acrid smell is unbearable. Bodi covers her mouth and nose with her hand. It takes everything she has not to throw up. Insects and rats find a happy home here and she is trying not to think how many of those new companions are close by. Her eyes are streaming from the odour but also because she is petrified. She cannot be found. They are here. And there is nothing she can do.

Heavy footsteps pound above her head and she follows the sound of them coming down the stairs. Bodi can see her Mum is outside, almost in touching distance. Head down, surrendered to her fate, she looks weak and fragile. Dragging her feet, the Sick Boys hold her under each arm. 'Have they drugged her?' she worries. It takes Bodi all her effort not to call out. Inside her head her voice is screaming, 'Mum! Mum! I'm here!'

The Sick Boys' belts hold large, sheathed knives and batons. 'What can I do?' Bodi thinks, her mind racing and her palms sweating. 'Jump them? I'd be dead in a second.'

The Sick Boys are renowned for their brutal 'act first, ask questions later' approach. In fact, questions rarely get asked. They are the Presidents' private army of rent-a-thugs.

Her mum is shoved in the back of the van and the door slammed shut behind her. Bodi whimpers like a hurt puppy as she sees her mum disappear. The other guards get in the front and start the engine. Taillights disappear round the corner and then nothing. There is always an eerie silence following a visit from the Sick Boys. Curtains twitch but everyone stays indoors, lights turned low. No-one steps into to help their neighbours because you could be hauled off as well. Self-preservation is king.

Bodi sits down on who knows what. She thinks back over the day and desperately tries to piece together how this has happened. She wonders what alerted TrueSec to their where-abouts? Had someone ratted on them? Had she gone out one too many times? Was it her fault? They have gone for years un-detected, flying way under the radar and they have done noth-ing different in recent weeks.

She and her mum have been in hiding for as long she can remem-ber. They move round the same faceless blocks of flats every few months. It is easier for her to leave the house now as she is older and a similar height and build to her mum. As long as they leave separately then their neighbours are none the wiser that there are two of them. Ruby says that is the best way to keep her safe. Today Bodi had got the free pass, which is happening more and more these days as her mum retreats into herself. Without friends around her, Ruby has few anchors in the world. She floats off into her memories, of Bodi's father, of her younger self. Bodi finds it increasingly frustrating when her mum is like this, not hearing her, not engaging with the world. They have been at loggerheads for months, Ruby disappearing more and more and Bodi fighting with the confinement of their lives. But now Bodi wishes she had just stayed home and maybe she could have got them both out of there before it was too late.

Bodi waits until her neighbours' radios and TVs are blaring again before she ventures back to the flat. The door lock is broken, so she closes the door as best she can behind her, wedg-ing a chair against it.

Things in their living room are still fairly orderly, just an up-turned mug on the floor, which must have been dropped by her mum when the door was banged in. Bodi's mum had always known that this day would come and they were prepared. They merged their things so that it looked like her mum lived alone. One crumpled bed, few possessions, little in the way of furni-ture. Everything is just as she had left it a few hours ago except one important thing is missing. Her mum.

On the wall is their one piece of decoration: Ruby's "Map of Inspiration". Postcards and photos of her heroes that they take everywhere with them. Stuck on a well-worn poster of Rosetti's *Joan of Arc* are images torn from magazines and postcards of heroes from Charles Dickens to David Bowie, Frida Kahlo to Wonder Woman. Right at its heart is a postcard of the statue of Boudicca and her daughters riding into battle that stands on Westminster Bridge. The warrior queen of the Iceni that Bodi is named after. This is the world they have created for themselves. The gods that they worship and the teachings that they follow.

Bodi goes over and touches the image of Boudicca. 'What now?' she asks her namesake. It is tatty from where she has done this so many times over the years, but it does not matter because she knows the image by heart.

Overcome by the day, Bodi falls into the bed, weeping into a pillow to muffle the sound. She feels bereft. Her whole body aches. She can't stay here. They have an emergency drill and she has to follow it. The building's caretaker will be in to clear the flat first thing in the morning, so she knows she has to get a grip and get out. But for a while she lies there, inhaling her mother's scent and exorcising her pain. She is a million miles away from the Bodi of that morning. In one way she is free for the first time. No-one knows she exists. She could just walk out in the night and start again.

They have an emergency backpack that they update every Sunday evening. Bodi has started to get complacent about this and has to be nagged repeatedly to carry out what she considers an unnecessary chore. At the first sign of light, Bodi pulls it out of the cupboard and scouts the room for anything else she wants to take. She does not know how long she will have until her next meal so she grabs an apple and a half-eaten pack of biscuits from the kitchen counter and drinks a glug of water from a bottle in the fridge. She takes down the Map, folding it along timeworn lines and slots it safely into the backpack. She picks out some dull, unremarkable clothes and puts them on. This is no time to stand out. She has to go unnoticed, that way she can avoid being picked up by the authorities. She keeps on her army boots but changes into black leggings, a t-shirt and a plain hoody. She plaits her hair tight and pins it up, pulling her beanie back on. She triple-checks the contents of her bag: Photos. Money. Underwear. Fake ID. Pocketknife. She bundles everything else into a black bin bag. All her precious and much-loved clothes have to go, along with her favourite books. It is heart-wrenching. Her whole identity thrown in a rubbish bag. Sixteen years trashed.

The terrifying thoughts of what might be happening to her mum right now drives her out of the door. Backpack in place, hat on and head down, Bodi walks out into the dawn light. She is on her own now and she has to get to safety. Reluctantly, she hides her bin bag of possessions at the back of the stinking rubbish room. It is the safest place for it. As she leaves the block she feels she is walking away from what is left of her childhood. She realises has to become a strong young woman and take care of herself. She has to find a way to free her mother without being found by the authorities. Pressed against her chest, under her hoody, her painted locket holds the key to her future but she has yet to prize it open.

Ever since she could remember Bodi has worn her locket. It isn't pretty. In fact she wears it under duress because it looks like a kid's craft project gone wrong. What it is, she realised as she got older, is an antique dipped in durgy pink paint and faded sequins. The paint has sealed it shut and she has kept it like that because she knows only to open it should "they" come. Bodi feels that she should go somewhere significant to open the locket and so she takes the road that leads to the heart of their city. It is still dark and the workers lowest on the food chain are her only companions.

Bodi sits at the foot of the statue, halfway down the steps to the disused subway. Only a few of the Underground lines run now since the bombings and fires. Ratty pigeons peck at used paper cups and cigarette butts. Tugboats pull containers of landfill along the river below. Big Ben chimes half past six in broken discords across the empty streets and above her head Boudicca's black stallions charge their continual assault against the former Houses of Parliament. Once a stalwart of democracy, the great building's gothic remains stand jagged and charred against the orange glow of the approaching dawn.

She tugs back the corner of the fly posters that have built up a thick protective layer around the base of the monument. She can just make out the beginning of the phrase that she knows so well. "Boudicca, Queen of the Iceni, who died in AD61 after leading her people against the Roman invaders."

When she was small Ruby would hoist her out of her pushchair to run her fingers along the indentations of the golden letters. 'Here my little warrior queen.' She would say. 'Drink in her power and her beauty. See how blood can be so strong that you will do anything to revenge wrongdoing against your family. I would take on an army for you, if anyone hurt you, a legion of soldiers, just like her.'

'Horses!' Bodi would squeal and made a "clip clop" noise with her tongue. She had so loved those horses. Only now does she understand the significance of her mum's words. She knows that Boudicca the Iceni Queen had taken on thousands of Romans and their allies and slaughtered them to avenge the attacks on her daughters. She was no saint, she had plenty of blood on her own hands, but she had avenged their suffering the only way she knew.

Bodi takes her locket off and starts chipping away with a penknife to open it. As much as she hates the look of this thing it is laden with huge sentiment and she does not want to break it. Its ugliness belies the power it contains. 'Information is power', was another of her mother's mottos. 'But use that power wisely,' she would add. She sits for a few minutes tentatively chipping away; registering that sitting in one of the most public places in the city is not the most inspired idea. She gives it one last jab and it flies apart scattering its contents on the pavement. She grabs at them and scuttles down the steps to the underground station and leans in the large, gated doorway. Hands shaking she looks again at her hoard. The locket's centre is a glorious old gold, like nothing Bodi has never seen before, inside it sits a folded piece of translucent paper. She sits rigid, cradling the tiny amount of hope she has left in her hand. Like a tiny bird only she can revive and she prays to all the higher powers she can muster that this will hold the answers. Bodi unfolds it carefully. It has been in there a long time and she senses it could easily dissolve.

On one side is a list of names and addresses, on the other is written the following:

My sweet Boudicca
If you are reading this then I am gone. They have found me. I hope that it is when you're old enough to take care of youself. The alternative I can't bear to consider. These people here were my friends, as true a family as I could wish for. There when I needed them. I've done my best to give us our independence, but if I'm not around they are the only ones I trust to help you. Get to them and they will keep you safe.
Be careful with these names Bodi, as it would do irreparable damage if they were to get into the wrong hands. Do not try to find me, it will only endanger you.
Remember, I love you forever and always,
Ruby xxx

Bodi turns the paper over to look at the names but they do not register. One thing she knows, without a doubt, to a man they were all members of the underground movement Populus. The phrase "Do not try to find me" resounds in her head. How can she not? How can she accept she will never see her mother again? Her whole world has collapsed within the space of twelve hours.

'You alright kid?' She looks up, a crowd is forming and that isn't good. She stands up shakily and forces a smile.

'Fine, fine thanks. Erm, just dropped some change,' she says.

Bodi walks through the crowd trying to compose herself. The crowd disperses instantly, everyone has their own troubles to deal with. Bodi can still feel eyes on her, she turns back to the bridge to see if she is being followed but everyone is walking away. 'Just being paranoid,' she thinks.

That is it then, she will have to ask this new "family" what to do next. She sure as hell doesn't know what else to do. All she has to do is track them down. Just that one huge, dangerous thing. Locket thrust deep in her pocket, she glances quickly at the first address and sets off north, away from the river.

Despite being confident in herself, Bodi is not exactly brilliant with new people. Not that she is a recluse, but her situation means she has led quite a secluded life. She never got to set down roots because they moved around so much. Her mum had left Populus when Bodi was around three and had broken all ties – or so Bodi thought – and consequently Bodi is pretty nervous about what she might unearth. Her mum rarely goes into why they left, she always says it was for the best and that Bodi is better off. 'We stand a greater chance on our own'. That was what she said. Very cryptic. There are certain things she knows not to push with her mother and this is one of them. Well, this is the biggest of them. If she is honest that is why she is quite surprised that her Mum suggested she find them. Bodi never thought that Populus would be part of her life, just a painful episode in Ruby's.

Populus holds mythical status among the lower classes of the city. It is hard to determine what is truth and what fiction about their exploits. Their leader, Clement, disappeared once they conceded to the President's military forces. Disappeared rather than died is the general consensus, but again, who knows? There is always talk that Populus will reappear to take on the system, but over time faith in this had waned. People are divided on what good they had achieved. Had Populus' actions inched them ever closer to the breadline? They lived in a blame culture. It is easier to blame someone else for your situation than take responsibility and Populus's own violent actions means it is an easy, faceless target.As word got out about the inhumane treatment of those that spoke out, the public came to accept that they had absolutely no say in the future of the city. Confidence in change vanished and they trudged begrudgingly through ever-insular lives. Daydreaming edged further off the agenda. Posters of the President were plastered everywhere telling them they had never had it so good. Those that were torn down were replaced by ten more. The country is in more than a slump. It is face down and drowning in a dirty, shallow puddle.

Bodi has been walking for a while. She is surprised she has drawn little attention despite the desperation written large across her face. She has no poker face despite her best efforts. Her mum always knows when she is lying. She pulls her beanie further down and hands in pockets marches on. She checks her tatty AtoZ. The first address is in Camden.

When she finally arrives at the home of 'Nancy', the tower block looms above her like an aggrieved spectre. Bodi climbs nine flights of stairs to the flat, pulling herself up the last two by the hand rail, to discover not only is no one home but there is no home. There are no windows or doors, not even the metal shutters of an abandoned house. She can see from one side of the building right through to the open air. Wrecked by the elements and covered in graffiti and addicts' old needles, this is not somewhere Bodi wants to hang about so she runs down the stairs two by two. When she gets to the ground she is totally out of breath and bent double she staggers down the road.

Bodi feels panicked by how much she is losing control and as much as she tries to focus on moving forwards she feels a huge pull back to their old flat. But she knows from years of moving, that forward is the only direction available to her. And their old flat isn't that anymore, she has to accept it. It is just an empty breezeblock box waiting to be filled with the secrets of another desperate family.

Bodi can't believe it when she looks at the next address on the list. Marylebone. She had pretty much gone past it on her way here and could have gone there first. She isn't thinking straight.

Rationale has been replaced by adrenaline-fuelled panic. She keeps trying to put thoughts about what is happening to Ruby to the back of her mind but every time she finds her focus horrific images flood into her head. Images of torture and beatings. Images of her mum slumped in the corner of a cell. No one to call and no one to turn to. The sound of her mum's voice telling her not to go looking for her. 'Well, I'm not looking for you,' she thinks. 'I'm looking for Populus. And they can look for you. That's not entirely the same thing.' She convinces herself anyway.

Her legs ache from the long walk back south towards the river. Bodi stands opposite the second house on the list. It sits square in the middle of a small terrace, this time with its windows and doors intact. A mother walks past her in a daze, shush-shushing the baby screaming in a pushchair. Bodi manages half a commiserative smile, then spots a familiar black van turn the corner towards her so she heads down a side street. Heart pounding, she waits round the corner until they have passed and then retraces her steps. Knocking at the door she is met with half a woman's face peering from behind a chained door. She remains silent, her one visible eye staring through Bodi.

'Pierre?' Bodi asks.

'Do I look like bleedin' Pierre to you?' she snarls.

'Is he here?' Bodi tries again, already sensing the answer.

'Gone. Long gone. If you see him, tell him I need rent money.' She slams the door.

Bodi isn't that surprised by the woman's behaviour. Anyone asking questions to do with Populus can't expect a friendly welcome. But she is out of options. She knocks on the door again. A few seconds later the same face appears.

'Seriously?' she glowers.

Bodi hears the chain slide back and the woman opens the door quickly, startling Bodi who steps back and trips over her own feet. She lands head first in the gutter, catching her head on the kerbstone. 'Owwww.' She howls. The pain is like nothing she has ever known.

Before she knows it the woman is beside her and Bodi holds up her hands to shield her head. 'Please! I'll go! Just leave me alone!' she wails. But the woman just sits down next to her, pulling her up by her armpits to sit on the kerb with her. She uses the cuff of her jumper to wipe Bodi's face which is smeared with mud and soggy leaves.

'You're in a bit of pickle,' the woman says, much kinder now. 'Don't worry, nothing broken.'

Bodi bends double, her face crumpled with sadness. She can't get the words out. Just the odd 'Mum...gone...alone...' in between heavy sobs. The woman simply sits there and nods reassuringly. There is no way she can understand what Bodi is saying with all her words caught in blubs, but she rubs Bodi's back and tells her everything will be okay.

'Pierre?' she asks again. The woman shakes her head. Her face looking as sad as Bodi's.

The growl of the Sick Boys' van returning brings them back to reality. The woman runs back into the house with a quiet 'Sorry', and Bodi has no choice but to get up. Scuttling round the corner she finds a small park nestled behind the house. She hides under an old slide, resting her bruised cheek against the cold metal which goes some way to numbing the pain. The physical pain, at least. Curled up like a wounded animal, the reality of her situation hits Bodi hard. 'What if no-one is home, anywhere?' she wonders. 'What if all I get is slammed doors, or no doors, and I am completely utterly alone. What am I going to do? How am I going to eat? Can I sleep here, under a slide?' She almost laughs. Her situation is beyond absurd.

Bodi hugs her knees to her, trying to find some comfort. She feels the pressure of the locket against her collarbone. 'There are two other addresses on Mum's list. Two other possibilities, not none. It's not over yet.' She talks herself into keeping moving. She feels an overwhelming pressure to slump down on a bench and give in to defeat. But inside her is a force, a drive that her mum has instilled in her. She will not give in. Bodi stands up and faces her future head on.

* * *

Bodi wakes up to a cup of hot tea in Sam's library, next to the bug-infested kitchen and the miniature Amazon Jungle. She sniffs the tea first, just to make sure, but it smells normal enough. She takes a sip. It is sweet and though she doesn't take sugar it is just what she needed. A small reassurance that she isn't in a complete hell on earth. There is also a bunched up tea towel next to her, slowly dripping. She prods it and realises it is full of ice and she holds it tentatively to her throbbing eye. She bites into some cold toast but it makes her whole face ache.

She can hear Sam's voice booming way off in the house somewhere, who knows who to and what about. Parakeets flap and squawk outside and she tries to piece together the last few hours. Keeping her bag with her, she sets off to find a bathroom and finds a tiny one under the stairs, also stacked floor to ceiling with old paperbacks and magazines. She ducks into it and looks into the tiny mirror tacked on the wall. She splashes cold water on her face and takes another look, running her fingers through her hair and re-tying her plaits. The purple of her black eye is spreading down her cheek like sea fog.

'What am I going to do now in this house of strangers?' she wonders. She has to find her mum soon or within days she will be lost in the system and they will be separated forever. She checks a clock in the hall which means, if it is right, it is around nine o'clock at night.

Bodi hears strains of a song she recognises coming from upstairs and follows the music, singing along without thinking. Her childhood had been full of music and it soothes her to hear the rustling crackle of the grooves and small scratches under a worn needle. She comes to a half-open door on the first landing and stands still for a while just listening. There is no other sound coming from the room but the lilting reggae. She pushes the door open and sees that it is Reed's room. He is sat on his bed reading.

Inside the walls are covered in images of Populus, floor to ceiling: newspaper cuttings, articles torn from magazines, snap-shots, images recovered from old reels of film. There are posters showing newspaper headlines in huge letters, taken from seller's booths, blaring "London under attack" and banners from marches stapled to the ceiling. Not one patch of wallpaper or paint shows, like inhabiting a graphic trauma. Bodi stands wide-eyed not really understanding what she's seeing.

'I know this song,' she says, making him jump.

Reed looks up at her from under his curtain of hair.

'Can I come in?' she asks apprehensively.

'I guess you can,' Reed doesn't seem altogether convinced this is the best idea. She starts to leave the room. 'Sorry, sorry' he says. 'Of course, yes, come in...I'm not that used to visitors, that's all.' He gestures for her to come in.

Bodi smiles at him, glad of common ground. 'You and me both. You've moved around a lot too I suppose. Hard isn't it?' she says, still making small talk while wondering what she is surrounded by.

Reed nods and looks down, his rings knocking together on clumsy fingers. Bodi takes in the barrage of text and images surrounding her.

'All this is about Populus? All of it? Hey, you're like their biggest fan!' She tries not to sound too sarcastic. And fails.

'It's not what it seems,' he says defensively and gets up from his bed to try to leave, gesturing that she should follow him, but something familiar by the window catches her eye. She pushes past him, brushing his arm with her shoulder, and bends down to stare at a newspaper clipping. The newspaper has been torn roughly but Bodi can make out a woman clinging to the reins one of the horses at the front of the statue of Boudicca. She holds a huge striped flag aloft, her eyes to the sky, she is shouting euphorically. What the black and white image doesn't show you is the flaming red of the woman's hair blazing behind her. Bodi turns, looking at Reed close up for the first time, confused.

'Is that my mum?' she asks. Reed stands up to his full height, he brushes his fringe to one side and looks straight at her with his dark brown eyes. She is taken back by how intense his stare is.

'Yes, that's Ruby. You haven't seen that before?' he is amazed. 'It's just that's well, you know, *the* iconic picture, of Populus. Did she never tell you about it? Or about any of what happened? It was a pivotal day.'

Bodi turns back to the picture, searching for answers.

'I was just there today,' is all she can manage to say.

Sam interrupts them with a theatrical cough. 'They seemed to know you were coming. The guys at Populus.' Bodi wonders how long he has been standing there. He leads them both downstairs and walks through to the kitchen.

'So the meeting will happen first thing tomorrow.' He says. 'I suggest we eat this delectable feast and then hit the hay.' He gestures towards the bowls of rice, green beans and soy sauce on the table. Noticing she still has hold of her backpack, Sam smiles and said 'You can put that down Boudicca, we won't nick it.' She puts it by her feet but sticks her foot through one of the straps just in case.

'We should probably find you somewhere else to stay. I'm not sure it's right that you bunk in here with us two fellas, no matter how handsome we are!' Bodi catches Reed giving his uncle a mortified look. Sam shrugs it off. 'Well, first things first. We'll see how the meeting goes and what the next moves are and sort the whole 'where I lay my hat' thing out tomorrow. Dig in.'

Sam is trying his best to keep Bodi's spirits up but he is fighting a losing battle.

'My mum, in that picture. Were you there too?' Bodi asks.

Sam seems reluctant to discuss this with her.

'We really love Ruby, girl. We're going to do all we can to get her back for you,' he says.

'I don't mean to be rude, but that's not what I asked,' Bodi says stubbornly.

Warily, he responds, while chewing on a bean. 'Yes, I was there. It was a very special day. It was quite near the beginning of the cause, an earlier, happier time. We were all so high on possibility.' He sighs. 'We really thought we could change the world. It was just a peaceful protest at first and Ruby was caught up in the energy of it all. I don't think she ever thought for one minute that it would make her the poster girl for the campaign. It caused no end of problems that picture and it really was just youthful exuberance. Her parents wouldn't see her you see, after that. And Populus, well, they wanted to exploit her potential for their own ends.'

'Typical!' Reed interjects, fuming. Sam shushes him. Bodi realises she has misjudged Reed. He isn't Populus' fan boy after all.

'It was different then Reed, we were carefree and idealistic. Just young I guess. Young and in love with the idea of a new utopia. And now here we are, all in hiding, or dead. Not much of a utopia is it?' Sam says sourly.

'Do you think they're hurting her? Torturing her?' Bodi asks timidly. 'Do you think...do you think she could be dead?!' Bodi finally articulates her biggest fear. The one she has done her best to suppress since the Sick Boys had taken Ruby away. She feels nauseous and angry and weirdly static, all at the same time. Sam looks at the table, shrugs a little and shakes his head. Reed looks at her wide-eyed and she glimpses his own pain. 'What had happened to him?' she wonders.

They eat little. Bodi knows not to ask anything more. She knows from her mum that when Populus comes up it is best not to ask everything at once. They eat in silence then Reed shows Bodi to a tiny room where he has made up a bed for her.

'Tomorrow then?' he says gently.

'Tomorrow,' she replies in a whisper.

*R*uby felt her mobile buzz in her pocket and knew it was time to leave. She dumped the spray can in her bag, her latest masterpiece would have to wait. She hated leaving anything half-finished but she had already been grounded that month and she couldn't face being holed up in that creepy house again. She stood back to take in her progress.

'Aren't you going to tag it?' a voice said behind her. She jumped out of her skin. This wasn't part of the plan. She was normally good at getting in and out without anyone spotting her. She turned to see a guy around her age, tall, slim, his baseball cap on backwards skimming his black fringe to frame his face. He smiled at her as she blushed and waved a can at her in solidarity. She could relax. She was in good company.

'Gotta go,' she said and went to pick up her bag. He ignored her and handed her his can. She shrugged and then deftly tagged the corner.

'Devil Child? Hm, interesting.' He rubbed his chin like a pseud in an art gallery. She added two horns to the 'D'. 'Nice touch' he said, grinning. She handed him the can back with a small bow.

She thrust her hand forward, ever geeky when she should be cool, and quickly withdrew it. Manners maketh the man and all that but it wasn't very 'street'. The boy laughed. He put out his fist for her to bump, which she obliged hesitantly knowing she would get it wrong. 'Calder,' he said.

'Ruby,' she replied, looking everywhere but into his incredible green eyes.

He turned to go. 'See you in hell, Devil Child,' he said over his shoulder. She watched him lumber away, his legs were crazy long and he had a carefree gait. All in all it made for a seriously pleasurable sight. Ruby grabbed her bag and ran down the street. She would have to hop on the last tube if she was going to make it home before her mum got back from whatever work event she had that night. She popped into a corner shop on the way and picked up a bag of crisps and a bag of sour sweets. 'Dinner of champions!' she thought. She eyed the cigarettes behind the counter but she had been trying to quit so sugar would have to be her one indulgence.

The sugar high kicked in just as she got to the escalators and she *raced down them ignoring the 'please take care' signs everywhere. The world had gone health and safety mad. The doors were shutting on her tube but she bundled in just in time, giving a huge groan which the other passengers on the train acknowledged with a communal tut. Not only because she was holding up the train but because she was so obviously a 'youth' of the time. Disrespectful, dressed like a gang member, obviously a yob.*

She flopped into a seat and put her bag on her knee. Something was sticking out of the outside pocket. She pulled it out. A card with a giant P on it and an email address. How had Calder managed that trick?

A calling card. Very old school. She twiddled it with her fingers, itching to get home and get on her laptop. No way was she going to let that one walk away again.

TUESDAY

Bodi sleeps fitfully, fighting a barrage of nightmares, and wakes early to the sound of Sam's bone-rattling snores. On her way to the kitchen she creeps past Reed's room. Listening at the door she hears nothing. 'Is he as quiet asleep as when he is awake?' she wonders. 'Amazing he can sleep in there, considering the insanity lining the walls.' Tiptoeing quietly from one cold kitchen tile to the next, she pours herself some water from a bottle in the fridge. The world is asleep, the birds are singing a tender morning chorus and the sun is just coming up in a cloud-free sky. Under other circumstances she would think it quite a blissful way to see in a new day.

She sits at the table staring out of the window, her feet pulled under her on a rickety kitchen chair. Any sense of calm is annihilated by anxiety. Thoughts ping round her head like angry ballbearings in a pinball machine. About being here, where her mum is now, about meeting Populus, about time escaping her before she can rectify things. Her insides feel like a rope being twisted by giant hands.

She takes in the room, free of its household. Other than the obligatory stack of washing up and a crowd of glass bottles, there is nothing very masculine about the room. Saggy festoon blinds hang above the window and sun-mottled wisteria climbs the wallpaper. Some books have escaped the library but only as far one wall and the others hold pots and pans, crooked picture frames and even some ceramic bowls of long past-it pot pouri. Bodi wonders if Sam had inherited this feminine decor with the house or if a woman had tried to make her mark on Sam's life. Questions for another day. She looks at the clock. Two hours till the meeting, she had better get ready to meet this 'true family' of her mum's.

A half-awake Reed clambers through the alley and then walks Bodi to the meeting. Sam thinks it is safer if he takes another route, so has left before them and hopped on a bus. If they are caught with him then it could be difficult to extricate themselves from the situation. Bodi agrees to the plan though thinks it a little futile as they are all going to be in the same room in a matter of minutes. Still, she wants to humour Sam. She is warming to him as he has been nothing but kind to her since she arrived. Neither Sam nor Reed will tell her where they are going. Sam had insisted over breakfast that it is very much 'need to know' so now Bodi is tagging along with Reed, like any other couple of teenagers. Her guard is still up, niggled that she keeps finding herself in situations where she isn't in control.

Reed's stature grows as soon as he leaves the house. He walks with purpose and is considerably taller than she thought. His skin is the lightest brown and his black hair has a small patch of white at the back. His hands grasp the ends of his jumper in fistfuls, not in a shy way, but more like he is ready to run at any second. On edge, he is aware of everything and everyone around him. Along the journey Reed steps around her to ensure he is always the one walking on the outside of the pavement, nearest the traffic. 'Must be something he learned from his uncle,' Bodi thinks, intrigued by old-fashioned habits in a person of her age. She finds it a bit bewildering, if very sweet.

Bodi is fizzing with anxiety but wants to talk to keep her mind off things. 'Start small,' she thinks.

'How long have you lived with Sam?' she asks Reed casually.

'About three years. My dad was really ill with pneumonia and with all the moving around and not enough money, we couldn't get him treated properly. He died.' He says it very matter of fact. Bodi stalls slightly but Reed keeps moving. He is really pounding the pavement and she is struggling to keep up. She hadn't thought through what a can of worms a question like that could be. She realises that if she was asked something similar right about now, small talk is probably the last thing that would come out of her mouth. She tries to catch his eye, to convey her sympathy, but his eyes look anywhere but at her.

'He was only in his forties,' he adds, again very bluntly.

'How awful for you. And your Mum?' Bodi asks, thinking: 'If you're opening the can you might as well go the whole way.'

'She's always been gone, well pretty much. She found Populus too much. But she also had to leave when all non-nationals got kicked out. Mum and Dad weren't married so she had to go back to Japan. It's been hard keeping in touch,' Reed fidgets with his jumper. 'To be honest I don't remember her that well but dad always told me I looked a lot like her, particularly when I frown. Quite weird that, looking like someone you don't really know.' His sadness about this absence can't be masked by bravado. His brow furrows that distinctive frown and he can't contain a sigh. It is obviously quite a normal state for him in contrast to Bodi's naturally, often irritating, perkiness. She tries purposefully to look more sombre, wondering if her life in hiding has made her less empathetic. But feeling empathy can mean opening the gates to your own titanic emotions and she has learned it is shrewder to keep those gates firmly locked.

'Your mum, my dad.' Bodi agrees. 'Hard isn't it, because you miss someone who was never really around in the first place.'

'Dad was devastated when she had to leave.' They stop for traffic and Reed says little more. Bodi crosses her arms and resists the urge to whistle. It's like inappropriate behaviour is always a hair's breadth away with her.

'And now it's me and Sam.' Reed says.

'And Populus?' Bodi questions.

'Kind of. Dad warned me not to trust them. He'd say they were good people. But they're idealists. And that doesn't make for a 'happy reality'.'

'But your room,' she says.

'It's not a shrine to Populus. It's me trying to work out where I fit into all of it. More what were they thinking when they were doing those awful things? Do I belong with them? Am I one of them?'

'Can Sam help you?' Bodi asks. 'Does he talk about what they did?'

'Sam has some great stories but they're sea dog's tales. I think he got into it mostly for the ladies – his word - and the buzz of the fight. He liked the partying after a good brawl. By nature he's a cad, a joker, not really a mercenary. And age has made him quite mellow.' He smiles at the thought of his uncle. 'When I got to his house I was so angry and wanted to hurt Populus for what they did to my parents. But Sam has found a way to slow me down, to get me to consider all the angles. So I started to research everything rather than going in fighting. Sam said: 'You're more powerful working from the inside out. Stealth! Like a ninja!' Sam laughed so hard at that one that the birds squawked for hours.' Reed laughs too and his normal overwrought look evaporates from his face.

'Yeah, the birds, right?! So weird. And you can't even eat them!' Bodi feels herself flush as the words come out. She sounds moronic. Reed gives her a hesitant 'Er, okay' and that is that. End of conversation. They cross the road. Bodi red from head to toe, crushed at how she ruined their chat.

They walk the rest of the way in silence, stopping for traffic, taking an avid interest in the stores they pass. Bodi thinks about what he said. She certainly doesn't trust these people. Her mum has done her level best to keep her away from them but right now they are her only option for getting her back. How does that make sense? How far is she prepared to trust in what her Mum had written on a note who knows when? She is starting to doubt her own judgement.

Reed stops by a faded wooden sign that reads "St James's."

'Peculiar that such a secular group meets at a church,' Bodi thinks, perplexed.

They go to a side door and Reed leads her through the pews. The space feels lifeless, the air deadened with dust. There is no joy here, no praise the lord and 'morning has broken'. It is freezing, dirty and abandoned. The altar cloth is gone, no chalice, no swinging incense or Sunday schools. Religion, for the few that want it, is now served mostly through the radio. People have lost faith, and the absence of glorious pomp and ceremony make churches less welcoming. Bodi crosses herself, she isn't all that religious, but it is one of her self-created superstitions. She habitually crosses herself when she walks by a church or sees a funeral cortege. She tries to do it without attracting attention. She's not ready to confess her peculiar quirks.

She follows Reed to the back of the church through the vestry to a smaller wooden door. Behind the door are steps down into what Bodi assumes is the crypt. Her heart races like a jazz rhythm section but Reed is so matter of fact she doesn't have a minute to think what she is doing. He has obviously done it so many times before it has become a normal thing for him. Panic rises in her throat but she gulps it down.

Reed takes a torch out of his pocket and she follows him hesitantly. Descending into the crypt evokes every creepy cliché you can imagine: creaking stairs, cobwebs in her hair and a foul smell of damp. She keeps up with Reed and his great strides; she doesn't want to be left down here alone. He walks ahead and turns into another smaller room. Inscriptions line the walls, flagstones radiate a freezing chill up through her boots. Bodi daren't touch anything, clamping her arms tight to her sides. She goes to ask a question. 'You…' Reed cuts her off, holding his finger to his lips, shaking his head for her not to speak. So they venture further into the darkness. They aren't under the church anymore. Bodi realises her exit strategies are redundant now.

Thirty seconds later they reach a dead end. Reed points upwards and starts to climb up a ladder, pushing open a door when he reaches the top. Bodi stands there looking up, wondering what on earth she has got herself into. 'As if the tunnel isn't weird enough, now there's a trap door?! What is this? Houdini's mansion?' she thinks.

She takes a deep breath and climbs up, brushing the dirt off her hands when she reaches the top. Reed puts the trap door down behind her while Bodi takes in the scene. It is a huge room with vaulted ceilings and frosted glass. Solid wooden counters are edged in scuffed up grey carpet. What little daylight there is struggles to get through the dirt on the windows. Security cameras hang by wires off their high perches like long-dead birds.

'Where are we?' she asks.

'I can't tell you that or I'll have to kill you.' Reed jokes. Bodi's eyes widen. 'It's an old bank.'

As they walk through the room Bodi trips up over another trapdoor in the floor. She bends down to look closer at the floor, there are a few of them dotted around. She nudges Reed and points at them, bemused.

'They lead to different buildings. I only know the route we came and my way out but Sam comes through a bookies. He definitely chose that on purpose. He likes to bet on the dogs. Everyone has his or her own route. We had to be quiet back there because that section of the tunnel goes under some houses.'

She walks across the room carefully. At the end of the corridor she sees a huge metal door. The vault? The irony of a group of anti-establishment vigilantes meeting in bank vault is not lost on her. This really is ousting the rich.

'A bank? Really?' she raises her eyebrows at Reed.

'Now Bodi, no one ever said that civil uprising can't be fun!' he quips. There is that other side to him.

Reed stands to one side with mock chivalry. 'After you.'

Bodi walks down the corridor with as much confidence as she can muster, which is about zero plus adrenaline, and with a hint of corny theatrics the door opens as she approaches. She steps over the threshold into the unknown. Time to meet Populus.

The group that is pouring over a huge map on a table stop what they are doing and as one go silent. Like hitting the mute button at the crux of the film. A few of them give her an encouraging smile but others just stare. There are around a dozen of them in the room. Bodi had expected more and is sad that they don't look a little more imposing. The vault has been cleared of its contents but the room retains the particular smell of paper money and it feels like there is not quite enough air in the room.

Sam steps forward and Bodi nods hello.

'Miss Boudicca. Glad to see you survived the journey. Confess your sins on the way in did you?' He chuckles. 'Bit spooky I know, but needs must and all that. Guess I should do some introductions.'

Taking her hand, he walks round the table. He comes to a small, round woman with glasses, dressed in a colourful array of mismatched Indian clothes, her grey streaked hair sticks out, like Einstein in drag. She is one of the few welcoming people, so Bodi smiles back.

'This is Morag, and Morag's brother Fergus.' Sam says. An almost identical slightly rounder, slightly more conservatively dressed man nods at her.

A taller, slim woman with styled, long, blonde hair looks Bodi up and down. Sam introduces her with some reverence: 'Penelope.'

'And my daughter, Felicity.' Penelope adds, with the aggrandised tone of a stage school mother.

A girl around the same age as Bodi steps forward from behind her mother. She is as tall as her and as blonde. Her eyes widen, looking her up and down. Her supercilious look quickly turns to disinterest and she turns and walks away. Penelope doesn't bat an eyelid at her daughter's rude behaviour, simply holds her forced smile. Beads of sweat start to form on Bodi's top lip, and she feels like Penelope is relishing in her discomfort.

Sam squeezes Bodi's hand and hurries on through the group, reeling off a tumble of names, some of which she recognises from the note inside the locket. Hatty. Mo. Pierre. The infamous Pierre of the missing rent! All the while Bodi is aware of Reed standing just behind her by the door. From there he can watch everything that is going on in the room. Sam stops listing names when he reaches the end of the table where two remaining men stand in close discussion. Sensing the quiet, they both turn to face Bodi as one. The elder one walks towards her his hands outstretched. He has neat, short dreadlocks and is wearing a military outfit a hair's breadth from a tin pot general. His immaculate tailoring stands out among the rest of the group's threadbare ensembles. Bodi guesses he is probably the same age as her mum. His solemn face breaks instantly into a welcoming smile, but one that Bodi is nervous of. It feels disingenuous.

'It's so wonderful to see you again Boudicca. We've been expecting you but I do wish it were under better circumstances.' He pauses and takes her in – her dirty hair, her grey skin, her fraught expression. 'I'm sure we can do something to rectify that very quickly.'

Sam moves away from Bodi's side, Reed steps back a little as well. It is like this man is surrounded by his own personal force field.

He stands right in front of her and put both his hands on her shoulders. 'My name is Balthazar. You are very welcome.'

'Balthazar? Okay. Hi. Thanks. How are you?' Bodi gabbles her words, trying to avoid his gaze. He turns her by her shoulders to her right and steps back.

'And this, is my son, Evan.' Bodi looks at him and then instantly lowers her eyes. She works her gaze up from his feet. He has a similar military sheen to his father's: boots tied tight, clean; pressed combat trousers; neat nails; a spotless jumper. He is stockier though and his face is different, a little softer, more of a baby face. A gold chain winks from under his collar. He has an earring. Bodi can tell he is trying to play the good son, trying to show he means business, but by rolling his eyes conspiratorially he reveals he too is finding it all a bit OTT. Evan holds his hand out to shake hers.

'Boudicca.' He smiles at her and she relaxes a little.

'Bodi?' she offers.

'Boo?' he challenges and she laughs, still holding his hand.

'Sure. Why not?!'

'We should get on with it, don't you think?' Reed interjects a little too loudly and Bodi drops Evan's hand. Everyone turns back to the table but there is just enough time for Evan to give her a quick wink, look past her shoulder and nod.

'Reed.' He says curtly. Reed bristles.

'Eva*nder*.' Now it is Evan's turn to bristle.

While Balthazar walks back to the head of the table, Bodi finally gets a chance to look at the map. It is the weirdest map of London she has ever seen. Gone are boroughs, postcodes and road names. In their place, symbols she doesn't recognise and lines drawn in red and black. Areas encircled and shaded in. 'Codes, perhaps? Safe areas?' Bodi has no idea and she doubts she is going to be wiser any time soon.

Morag starts. 'When they took me away, I was held in Highgate. In the rooms they had under the cemetery.'

'That was years ago Mor.' Her brother retaliates. 'There's no way they're using the same place now.'

'They may have come back to it.' Morag sounds hurt they are dismissing her theory.

'I think the less time spent on Morag's short-lived incarceration the better,' Penelope snips.

'I think we need to step away from conjecture.' Balthazar booms through the prattling. 'We need to follow their logic and see if anyone in the network has any intel on what happened.' At the word "intel" Sam gives him serious side eye. Balthazar catches him.

'Intel. Yes, intel.' Sam says, recovering. 'Very good Balt. Anyone? Any intel?'

Bodi looks round the table. Someone standing at this table has to have the answer to how to get her mum back, but who is it? Balt pulls her next to him.

'Where were you living Boudicca?' he asks. Bodi points on their map the rough whereabouts of their flat. It is hard to be exact with all their strange areas and codes. 'Turner Street. In Bateman House. We'd been there about a year, it was starting to feel permanent,' she says wistfully.

'Too long. Way too long.' Balthazar's tone is disapproving.

'But you get so sick of moving. You don't know anyone. You feel isolated,' she counters. Morag nods in agreement. 'We just wanted to feel a little bit of continuity.'

Balt sighs and continues his interrogation. 'Tell me exactly what happened.'

Bodi tells her story to Balthazar and the rest of the group. It is like recounting a dream where some elements are still extremely, painfully, vivid and others have begun to fade. Every so often Balt just stares at her, close-up, completely invading her personal space. Almost as if he stares hard enough some unknown truth will fly direct from Bodi's subconscious to his.

He pummels her with questions.

'Did you talk to anyone?...Give your mum away?...Had she developed any problematic friendships?...Boyfriends? You, her?... Why didn't you move more?... Why didn't you stay in touch with Populus? We could've protected you.'

Bodi thinks she knows the answers but she starts to doubt herself, second guessing what Balthazar wants to hear. Finally, just when she thinks she will start screaming and never stop, Sam steps in between her and Balthazar.

'Okay mate. Enough with the Stasi treatment.' He puts his hand on her shoulder and she feels instantly safer. 'Let's give Boudicca here a few minutes and see what 'intel' we have so far.' He isn't going to let that one drop.

The adults huddle round, closing Bodi out of the circle. Like they've stripped the flesh from her bones and are gathering to devour it. She retreats to the corner of the room to lick her wounds, her mind awash with possibilities. Highgate, Battersea, London Bridge. Where will they even begin? She rubs her sore eyes and her aching back, trying to stop feeling otherworldly.

'Why the hell do you even want to find her anyway?' The blonde girl Felicity shoots at her, interrupting her fumbling thoughts. Bodi hasn't even realised she is sat nearby.

'You what?!' Bodi is dumbfounded.

'At least you're free now. No one knows who you are. You're not involved in this hideous carnival of freaks. You can just be who you want to be. Go off into the world and be normal.' Felicity flicks her hair dismissively.

'But I need to find her. She's all I have.' Bodi says quietly, feeling very defensive about her relationship with her mum even to this awful girl. Then again, if *Penelope* was her mum she might think differently.

'You've got to wake up hon, once you get embroiled in all this crazy then that's you in hiding for the rest of your life. You should go off now before you get completely dragged down with it.' Contempt drips from Felicity's perfectly lip-glossed pout.

Reed walks over and pulls her up on her comment. 'What do you think is out there that you don't have here, Flip?' he challenges.

'God *Weed*, were did you come from? Lurking in the shadows, again? I was just saying to our new *friend* that she should get out now, while she still can. Don't you want that, to live like everyone else? None of this tunnels and plans and military BS. No plans to take back the city. As if they ever had any clue in the first place. They're all certifiable!' Flip's anger is tinged with disappointment.

'Well, let's say, for argument's sake..' Reed says.

Flip cuts him dead. 'What do you even sound like? You're not right in the head Weed. Take the dictionary out of your arse and go plot another spectacular fail with the Hit Squad over there.'

Bodi stands up between their face off.

'Flip, is it? You're completely delusional. It's too late already. No matter what Mum did to keep me away from you all, I'm fast realising I was always a part of it. I can't live a normal life. This *is* my normal.' She walks away from their squabbling, back to the table where the adults are still debating what to do. Bodi had begun the day putting her trust in these strangers to deliver Ruby safely back to her, but seems a little more hopeless now. She isn't entirely sure they have the answers. They are so hidden from real life is there any way they could know what is happening to her mum or where she is?

Sam takes the floor. 'We need people on the inside. I can't stress that enough.'

Bodi can hear Reed from earlier "Stealth! Like a ninja!" which makes her smile. She is starting to feel that she might have an ally in Sam.

'But who can get away with it?' challenges Morag 'They know all of us. Christ, we'd be carted away before you could say 'Evening Officer Dibble'.'

Bodi doesn't know what on earth Morag is talking about. What any of them are talking about and why they're not already *doing* something.

Bodi catches Evan's eye across the group, he's been listening in too. He steps to the head of the table and Bodi moves to stand beside him.

'Us?' he whispers.

'Us,' she replies conspiratorially.

Evan coughs and the group turn to him.

'There is only one way this is going to work. They don't know us. We should be the ones to go find Ruby,' he says, firmly.

The adults' protestations resound around the room. Their idea isn't going down well.

'You can be like our command post and we can infiltrate from inside. We'll just do what you say. We'll be your eyes and ears. Your chess pieces. Gathering intel and bringing it back to the group. *You* get to make all the decisions.' Evan knows how to get round them. It is all about making them think they hold the power.

'He's right.' Reed speaks up from the other end of the table. Evan looks surprised that Reed has his back.

Flip just stands agog. 'You've got to be joking! No way. I'm not getting involved in this, it's batshit.'

'You're always saying you want to live with the normals Flip. Well, this is your chance.' Reed baits her.

'Not while I have breath in my body will you be a part of this, Felicity,' Penelope's shrill tone rings across the room.

Well, that is settled. Nothing Flip likes more than to upset her mother. 'I'm in,' she whispers to Evan.

The adults are all talking over one another again. 'Can we let this happen?...They don't know the first thing about strategy... How would they protect themselves?... They're just kids.'

But Bodi knows. This is it. Her mind is alive with the possibilities. Her fingers tingle and she feels power course through her whole body. She feels stronger than she has done in 24 hours.

They are going to get her mum back.

Evan nudges her shoulder with his.

'Miss Boo. Our newest recruit.' He grins.

Bodi senses Evan has been waiting a long time for an excuse to get out into the real world and cause some havoc. He is practically dancing with joy. He leaves her to go talk strategy with Balthazar. Bodi stands there, tuning out the dissonant hubbub. She knows she can make this happen.

She can hear trap doors slamming. Populus' members disappearing back down the tunnels to their 'real' lives. Bodi stares at the map, waiting to leave. She puts her palm flat over where she and her mum lived. 'We're coming' she promises.

Reed comes up to her. 'We should get going. Everyone decided you should stay with us. If that's okay? Sam's has the most space and well, we thought it would be good not to move you around so much.' Bodi is grateful. She had worried she would be sent off to live with Penelope and Flip. A lose lose situation all round.

Bodi looks round the vault. They are the last ones there. Time to head down a tunnel again and see what rabbit hole they pop out of.

Ten minutes later Reed pushes aside some shelves and she finds herself in the cellar of a restaurant. Huge drums of cooking oil are piled high with bags of potatoes. Old chest freezers hum and churn out rancid, warm air. Reed walks up some grotty stairs and she follows him into a burger bar. The guy working behind the counter isn't at all shocked to see them and carries on talking to his customer. Reed helps himself to a portion of chips, salt and ketchup, and lets himself out through the front of the shop with Bodi behind him, agog.

The music was crazy loud but Ruby was happy for it to numb her skull. She swigged from her can and looked around for him. For the past hour she had tried to look nonchalant but now it was totally annoying her that she couldn't find him. She even considered lurking by the warehouse exit until he arrived/left but that really would smack of desperation. She hadn't been able to stop thinking about him all week and that was way unusual for her. So she made one more circuit of the room, dancing as she went, so as to not look the full stalker.

All of a sudden someone was shoved into her with huge force. She landed in a heap on the floor with this person on top of her. Some guy loomed over them both. 'I told you to stay away Cal. She doesn't want to see you anymore.' Seemed she was not the only stalker in town. The shover walked into the crowd and it felt like they sat there with him on her lap for quite a while.

'Cal?' she thought, pushing the body off her. He started laughing. 'Shit! Sorry,' he said, picking up his cap. Then 'Oh! It's you! Satan's

spawn!'

'Devil Child,' she said, never more embarrassed in her life.

'That's what I meant,' he laughed. 'You came. Amazing.' He looked genuinely happy to see her and reached down to pull her up.

'Ruby' she leant in and shouted in his ear. All around them the crowd was going insane as the music kicked off.

'What?!' he shook his head.

'Ruby. My name is Ruby.'

'I know.' She wasn't entirely convinced he did but she didn't care. He was still smiling that dorky smile and still holding her hand. 'Let's get out of here, Ruby. The music's lame anyway.' He pulled her behind him, round the edge of the room to the exit. Ruby wondered momentarily whether she should be worried about this other girl. Not like she was a real threat and something was definitely happening here.

He pushed the doors open and ploughed through a huge group of people. Ruby pulled her hand free to put on her hoody, instantly regretting it. 'What if he never holds my hand again?' She winced at the inanity of that thought. This was bad.

She kicked a can and sent it clattering down the road.

'You a pro footballer, like?' he ribbed.

'Yeah. On a million quid a game.'

'Minor leagues then.'

Calder turned with a jump and planted himself right in front of her. 'Funny that, me running into you here.'

'Well I'd say 'running into' is a smidge inaccurate,' she teased. 'What was that bloke's deal?'

'Ah, nothing, just big brother issues. I mean literally. Not like, 'Big Brother' but my ex's big brother. She's struggling to move on.' Ruby let this go, not really wanting to dwell on his ex.

'Good rave' she offered, weakly.

'Yeah. For sure.' He pulled the string on her hoody.

He looked down at her, still smiling, and took hold of either side of her top, guiding her backwards against the wall. A raver's slow waltz. He lifted her up on top of the wall and she yelped with glee.

'You came then?' he teased.

'It would appear so.' Ruby looked up at him from under her long eye-

lashes. That always did the trick.

Cal stood between her legs. Arms firm, either side of her. Ruby was happy to be trapped.

'Coincidental, of course.' he said, cheekily.

'Completely. Utterly. Coincidental.' she drawled.

And he leaned in to kiss her while the thud thud thud of the bass vibrated through them both.

WEDNESDAY

'Boudicca!' Sam tries to wake her. 'We've had word from one of Balt's contacts. They've seen your mum.'

'Whaaa?' Bodi is half asleep and sounds are barely registering, let alone words and meaning.

'Your mum, she's okay love. Well as far as we know.' Sam's smiling face looms over her. She forces her eyes open.

'Where is she how they know it's her how we get to her?' The words drizzle out of Bodi's mouth in a long mumble.

'She works at the central processing centre, Balt's contact. She saw your mum yesterday afternoon but she doesn't know where they've taken her. So good news. All well for now.'

Sam squeezes her arm then leaves the room. Bodi pushes herself up and leans against the wall. The sun is barely up and the fuzziness in her head starts to settle to an even hum. 'Processing? Processing for what?' Her mind runs away with the possibilities. Prison? Deportation? Execution?! 'You need to calm down,' she reassures herself, 'got to get used to the fact that nothing happens instantly around here. At least they know where she is.' She tries to bury each of these destructive thoughts, though shoots of negativity still break ground.

She wonders what passes for a bath in this house. If she is going to concentrate today it is better she doesn't smell like a baboon's bum. She tentatively pushes open doors along the corridor. One is entirely full of birdseed and smells beyond words. Definitely not something you want encounter on an empty stomach. Another is just full of tea chests, their contents pouring out over the floor as if Sam has been desperately searching for something that is in the very bottom of the tea chest at the very bottom of the pile.

Bodi eventually finds the bathroom. She sits staring blankly at the plughole as water heats up in an ancient hot water tank. The tiles are chipped and broken and what must have been pale blue wallpaper peels down from the ceiling. She feels relief that her mum is still alive and even though they can't get to her, it feels like they will. She hopes they will.

She thinks back to yesterday when they had got back to the house. Sam had sat alone with her in the leather chairs and patiently answered her questions about Populus. She knows it was a time that her mother had loved and that had defined her before she had been born, but it had also trapped her and taken away her freedom. Beyond that Bodi's knowledge is sparse.

'It was something that started out very positive.' Sam began. 'We were a force to be reckoned with. The arrogance of youth meant we thought we could and would achieve everything we set out to do. We felt oppressed and didn't like where the world was heading. The rich were getting richer while the rest of us couldn't get a shoe in. Not just that, the values of the country were all upside down. It was the culture of the ego. Instant fame and instant gratification. It's not that we were pushing for a new morality, far from it, but we were hoping that people would wake up to themselves. Wishful thinking as it turned out.'

'What sort of things did you do?' Bodi asked, not really wanting to know the whole truth.

'Well, you've seen Reed's room, love. Chaos, disruption, damage. A huge amount of damage. Upset, pain. That was never the plan but the end point was very different from where we started. We began as a small group allied to a larger cause. Populus is international but we were so consumed with London and changing what was immediately around us we didn't fully absorb what was going on elsewhere. They'd blow up a bus in Madrid and we'd think 'Well, that's not us. We would never do something like that. They must have some rogue members.' Blinkered and naïve. Well I was. And a lot thinner!' Sam patted his belly and chuckled. He was trying to diffuse the tension but Bodi didn't bite.

'After a while you start to believe that peaceful demonstration is not enough. You must make your mark. People became bored with us. In fact, we irritated them. And we had set out to be inspirational. Inspiration to irritant in a matter of months...

'You have to take back the headlines to reach them. So gradually those that are predisposed to violence start to get their way more and more and the original principles are abandoned. Soon you're the one helping to blow up a bus, or setting fire to a house, or ransacking an office block, and you convince yourself that it's for the greater good. But mostly you're just high on the attention and the adrenaline. For a bunch of veggie liberals it turned out we were huge adrenaline junkies!' Sam shook his head, embarrassed.

'What's the worst thing that you did, personally?' Bodi asked tentatively. Sam looks at her, with sadness in his eyes.

'I'm not going there, my young friend. I was a whole different person then and you wouldn't be sitting so cosy here with me if you knew the terrible things that I've done. I convinced myself that I was just there along for the ride. For the ladies, you know! The craic! But it became deep-seated and any sense of right and wrong I'd had before shifted. When we began we were true to our common beliefs. We genuinely were right about all of it. There needed to be a big shift in the status quo. But it turns out you've got to create a big stir to get things changed, so we really stirred things up.

'When we started out I never believed in a million years that we'd make things worse rather than make them better. And now, here we sit. My little brother Cal is no longer with us and your mum is gone and you have to question it all.' Sam shook his head. Bodi felt mixed emotions. She felt his loss, but it was hard to reconcile these actions with people who wanted to do good. And she was struggling to see Sam as one of them, let alone her mum.

'Do you think that we'll have to do some bad things? You know, to get Mum back?' Bodi doesn't think she can be violent. The thought of even slapping someone fills her with horror.

'I hope not, dear heart, because those things change you and you don't recognize yourself afterwards. And *you* are perfect just as you are.' He stood up and lifted up her chin with his hand. 'Never forget who you are, Boudicca Jones. Even in the middle of the chaos, try to remember.'

At that point, alone in a rambling house of books and birds and rooms plastered with anarchy, Bodi had made a promise to herself that she would never forget who she was.

Bodi takes a very shallow, quick bath, shivering all the while. She is glad to be dressed again and finds herself back at Reed's door. She hadn't got enough details out of Sam and she wants to know more. She knocks at the door and getting no answer opens it hesitantly. Dappled sunlight comes through the window, spots of light pinpoint different newspaper clippings. She follows their trail around the walls, reading stories and looking at photographs:

Populus protest camp set up outside Houses of Parliament, numbers swell to two thousand...So called Peace Camps have sprung up around London in parks and squares and are spreading to other cities across Europe...Twelve dead in underground fire, 30 injured... An unnamed source said "we won't stand for the hypocrisy of the government any longer, we had to take action"..."Populus are ruining London, I don't feel safe to go out anymore," said mother of two...Fire fighting units unable to cope with levels of arson...Populus targets government officials...Call for action, troops line the streets...Is marshal law a step too far?... Residents pack up and leave the city fearing for their safety...A special review board has been set up to look into army brutality..."I'm not sure who's worse Populus or the army," said one resident, "I feel like I'm a prisoner in my own home"...Special forces deployed to rid the city of Populus...An already stretched economy takes massive hits, The City is in freefall...'Burn them out, see how they like it' said Jack, 65 of Harrow...Special Forces take back the city, the hunt begins for ring leaders...

Around the room the story escalates from a few minor incidents to a full-scale battle on the streets of London. Some Londoners join the fight feeling more scared of the army and the law enforcers than they had been of Populus. Pictures show how Populus went from a well-intentioned protest group to being accused of every crime committed in the city.

Bodi's head is full of bodies, fires and fighting. Not only is her mum possibly responsible for killing people but she herself is now involved with the people who had let that happen. Made that happen, this isn't passive. 'Once I start down this road will I ever have any kind of a normal life? Is Flip right?' Bodi wonders, 'Should I get out now while I can? Is mum an arsonist? A murderer? How did she go from that carefree young woman on the front of the newspaper to being a mother on the run? Do I know her at all?' This is really challenging Sam's edict for her to remember who she was.

She looks at the heap of blankets on Reed's bed, like a nest they curl up round and round on top of each other. She sits in the nest. It is still warm and seems as safe a place as any to be. The text on the walls around her dissolves into more of a blur. 'Maybe if you don't look too hard you don't see it,' she thinks. 'Wouldn't that be nice?'

She notices a photograph pinned to the wall next to Reed's headboard. She pulls it off the wall. On the arm of a purple velour armchair sits Ruby, much younger, smiling, wearing a halter neck top and shorts. Next to her is Bodi as a toddler - shy of the camera, bare-chested wearing only pants, streaked in sun cream with a mop of crazy red curls. On the other arm sits a man with Reed's build and looking like a young Sam but not quite. Maybe Reed's dad, Calder? And right there, between him and Bodi, sits what can only be a young Reed, a reassuring arm around Bodi, bashed up trainers at the end of skinny legs. All big, dark eyes from under a solid bowl haircut with a huge grin on his face, just a little older than her. He has the sweetest smile, something Bodi has seen little of since she arrived. It is a tiny, worn snapshot of a happy day in the summer before Ruby had left.

'Reed knew me before?' Bodi leans into take a closer look, disbelieving.

'Er hello. Make yourself at home why don't you?!' Bodi jumps. Reed is back. Bodi waves the photograph at him, eyebrows raised in a 'what the hell?' fashion. Reed sits down next to her.

'So Bodi, the thing is, I've known you all my life. Just happens that I haven't seen you for, like, 14 years.' He tries a smile, at once transformed to a giant version of that gangly kid in the photo.

'Oh my god! Reed?! I feel like my head is exploding. You knew me all along and didn't say anything?!' Bodi pushes his arm but doesn't budge from where she is sitting, both their legs dangling off the edge of the bed.

'Come off it, we were just kids, Bodi. I didn't *know* you know you. I have a vague recollection. But that might just be because of this photo. Do you ever think that? Do I really remember this event or it just because of the photo?' Reed is going off on a tangent so Bodi puts her hand up to stop him. He sighs. 'We just have to use them Bodi, to get your mum back. Get your mum and leave, get as far away from them as you can. They're devastating. Everything they touch turns to crap. People die, people leave and people get taken away and it's entirely their fault. But if we use them to get through the first door, then we can work the system the way *we* want. Maybe we can make things okay again.'

'Yeah. I guess.' Bodi doesn't sound sure. Her brain feels like sugar being spun in a candyfloss machine. 'But you knew me...'

She doesn't move. They sit there for a few minutes like that on his bed. Reed leans against the wall awkwardly, occasionally pushing his fringe out of his eyes; Bodi can hear his breath quicken. What else wasn't he telling her?

Sam's yelling disturbs them. 'Kids! You better get going. Don't want to keep the great and all-powerful Balthazar waiting.' She can hear him whistling *We're off to see the Wizard* as he leaves the house.

It is getting colder. Bodi yearns for her red coat with the fur trim and to be walking through Green Park again without a care in the world. It seems like weeks since that was her life but it is only three days ago. Three days! She looks over at Reed, his head down as normal striding forward, but she is getting better at keeping up with him. They are off to work on the plan with Balthazar. Bodi isn't sure what to expect as she has only spent a matter of minutes with the man but he seems like he knows what he is doing. Of the Populus members that she had met yesterday she found him the most terrifying, but she soon realised that he was the man to get things done.

* * *

The sign by the door reads "Frank's Gym". Walking through the entrance she smells the sweat-drenched leather of the ring, the gloves and punching bags. The stink of disinfectant is an after note rising from the floors, but everywhere still looks grimy. Through a set of swing doors they come into a dark hall. At first it seems they have the place to themselves, then her eyes refocus. Strong spotlights light up the boxing ring in the centre of the room.

Balthazar sits cross legged in the middle of the ring with Evan facing him. They are silent with their eyes open, completely still. Flip sits to one side on a plastic chair pulling at split ends, bored. An old air conditioning unit grumbles its presence.

'Thank god you're finally here, now we can get on with it, whatever 'it' is.' Flip's clipped tones jar the calm. Evan shoots her evils and she glares back. Again Flip looks immaculate, cool even. She is wearing the neatest work out gear and a high ponytail. Her skin is flawless. Bodi looks down at her outfit. She has fast run out of clean clothes and living with two men doesn't help. She is sporting another pair of off-black leggings and a holey Ramones t-shirt she found in the room of packing cases. She fiddles with her hair, which she has braided into two bulbous plaits. Her hair is becoming more unruly by the day.

Without using his hands Balthazar rises silently from his cross-legged position and Evan matches him. Evan turns and does a small bow to Bodi.

'Miss Boo.' She grins back.

'Evan.'

Balt climbs out of the ring. 'Right! Team! Let's take action, my legion of intel gatherers. We don't have much time and there's a lot to do. Seats please trainees.' Balt gestures to a line of seats in front him as he paces up and down in front of them.

They sit down quietly, the four of them. Flip, Evan, Bodi then Reed. Reed and Evan refusing to look each other in the eye. Balthazar commands their attention and begins:

'What you will learn here today will be invaluable, not just in the coming days but in life. Humans only use around 20 per cent of their grey matter and are capable of super human strength if only they learn how to use all their muscles – body and brain – in harmony.'

Flip mock yawns. Another nasty look from Evan makes her sit quietly but she still rolls her eyes.

'If you channel your inner strength you will overcome more than you thought possible. We will come to details of the plan shortly. But first, Bodi come with me. I need to assess your skills.'

'I have skills?' Bodi thinks.

Balt takes her to one side and the others walk off.

'What do you do to keep in shape Boudicca?' Balthazar asks looking her up and down.

'I'm sorry?'

'What regime do you follow to keep in shape? Yoga? Calisthenics? Running? How do you channel your energy?'

Bodi looks confused. 'Clothes?' she jokes. Balt keeps staring at her. 'Okaaay. Not really big on all that exercise stuff.' She dredges her brain for something, anything, energetic. 'I walk a lot. That's about it.'

'Right. Let's try some self-defence and see what your reflexes are like. What's your reaction if I do this?' His hand comes at her face as if to slap her. She squats down in a crumpled heap.

'Seriously? You're going to *hit* me?! I've already got one black eye, I don't need a pair.'

'Boudicca, we have a day, *one* day, to give you some basic skills and then we have to send you out to fend for yourself.' He reaches down to help her up. 'If even a couple of things stick today then you at least have something up your sleeve should anything happen. These guys have all done this stuff since they were kids. It was essential they knew how to take care of themselves, but I guess Ruby had other priorities...'

That gets her back up. Bodi stands up and looks defiantly at Balt. 'Give it another go.'

This time when he goes for her she puts her arm up to block it. He shows her how to react to someone coming up behind her. How to step on their foot, push back with her elbow, put her hand between her throat and her attacker's arm. He shows her how to go for weak spots: knee joints, the groin, to push at the nose or gouge eyes.

'Can't I just carry something, to protect myself?' she asks.

'What? Like a knife? No Bodi. Anything like that can be a potential weapon for them to use against you. Say you have a small knife, fine if you can hang on to it. What if they get it from you? Then you're in a whole other hideous situation. Your mind is your best defence. What can you pull down on top of them? What escape route can you see? How can you block their path? Running is not cowardice, it's self-preservation. Okay, take five. Then we'll get going on some mental challenges.'

'So no to the knife then,' she mumbles.

Bodi collapses on a seat next to Flip who is by the ring watching the boys box. It doesn't take a genius to realize that Evan is thrashing Reed. But Reed isn't backing down. He moves round the ring defending himself but isn't on the attack.

'What's going on?' Bodi asks Flip.

'Testosterone,' Flip groans.

The rivalry between Reed and Evan rages like an everlasting storm.

'Come on man, give me a fair fight. This is ridiculous.' Evan is winding Reed up and Bodi can sense his anger is building. 'Can't you see? Is your girly hair getting in your eyes? You want me to get you an ickle hair clip?' Still nothing back from Reed, Bodi can't understand what he is doing. He looks like he could hold his own against Evan but he isn't fighting back. Bodi can't even deal with the fact that they are fighting at all.

Evan is still baiting Reed: 'Don't want to break a nail? Worried you might bruise that pretty boy face of yours? The girls are watching man, come on let's give them something to look at!'

Reed looks over to Bodi standing at the side of the ring. A punch from Evan catches him off guard and he stumbles back against the ropes. Bodi shouts out: 'Evan! That's really not cool.' Flip does a low whistle.

'Element of surprise Boo. Got to use everything around you to your advantage.' He shrugs, doing a smug body roll to celebrate his win. Bodi looks for some support: 'Flip?'

'Well, he's got a point.' Flip shrugs.

At that moment, a huge flying kick comes out of nowhere, hits Evan on the shoulder and lands him flat on his back.

Evan lies on the floor stunned, reeling from Reed's body blow.

'Where the hell did that come from?' he gasps.

Reed leans over him. 'Taekwando. I've read books on it and practiced by myself but never had anyone to use it on. Before now.'

Reed looks down at Evan, thrusting his chest forward, his eyes bulging.

'Element of surprise, boo.'

Reed climbs out of the ring and walks away. Bodi sits down in the chair again and puts her head in her hands. How on earth is this going to work with these two at each other all the time?

By now some other members of Populus have arrived. Morag takes Bodi aside and sits down opposite her.

'Right wee'un. Let's work out where your strengths lie. You seem to me to be super bright, but sometimes book smart doesn't quite cut it.' She is smiling and Bodi knows she means well but she feels like she is sitting an exam on a subject she had never even heard of, let alone studied. 'What do you think you might "bring to the table" so to speak?' Morag delights herself by making quotation marks with her fingers. Bodi wracks her brain and comes up short. 'What sort of skills do you need to infiltrate a maximum-security establishment to rescue your stolen parent?' she ponders.

Morag tries to help her along. 'When you were moving around with your mum, how did you find that? Did you get on with people, could you win over strangers?' Bodi thinks back to just a few days before when her life had been relatively normal.

'I always got on with people but we had to keep a low profile.' She answers. 'I didn't really have friends and we had to be careful what we said.'

Morag nods, this is something that unites them all. Once they lived as a bustling huge community, now they are left to hide alone. Bodi offers hesitantly. 'I'm quite good with languages I guess. I've never learnt formally. Mum's terrible at them so she couldn't teach me grammar and stuff. But I've always had an ear for them and picked them up along the way. We had a Polish neighbour when I was a kid and she'd watch me for Mum. Another one of our neighbours taught me some Punjabi. And you just hear so many languages where we live that it's hard not to pick them up. Tusing kiṭhong ho Morag? Where are you from Morag? Dobry wieczor Morag. Good afternoon Morag. Stuff like that.'

Morag's face lights up. 'That's great Bodi. People don't even get me when I'm speaking English so I'm jealous! That's a very useful skill. Not only for communicating with our friends on the inside, but for baffling those Sick Boy ninnies. Their languages skills are a bit limited to say the least. Der...' Morag's eyes bulge as she pulls the face of an idiot and laughs to herself. Bodi is beginning to think that everyone involved in this group is insane. 'How about other forms of communication? Did your mum teach you anything from her time with us?'

Bodi scans the room, hoping something will jump out at her. She isn't used to talking about what she is good at and it is unnerving. Obviously her mum just accepts her for what she is and she doesn't spend much time analysing her strengths and weaknesses. She has good hair? She loves science fiction? She can make a mean dinner out of a seemingly empty kitchen cupboard? None of these are particularly pertinent now.

Reed is talking to Morag's brother Fergus in one corner, looking over some old books. Across the room Flip is sat with Hatty and her face is a picture. She looks like she wishes she were doing shooting practice instead with Hatty as her target. Bodi is starting to feel wound up. While all this stuff is no doubt extremely useful, they are losing yet another day. Nothing is actually happening and her mum is still gone.

She is about to raise this with Morag when her attention turns to raised voices coming from the trainer's office. Balt is giving Evan a hard time but Bodi can't make out what he is saying. Balt is standing with his hand on Evan's shoulder, talking to him just inches away from his face. Evan stands stock still, eyes locked on his father's. Morag rests a reassuring hand on Bodi's arm. 'Quite intense our Balthazar,' she says. 'Been tough on Evan since he was a bairn. His heart's in the right place but I'm not sure Evan sees it like that.' Evan marches out the office and the door slams against the wall behind him. He heads toward the changing rooms.

'Evander! Get back here!' Balt is fuming.

'Don't worry dear. It's just father and son stuff. Been going on since time immemorial. The young stag challenging the old buck! Keeps Balt on his toes.' Morag goes off to get a cup of tea.

Bodi leans her arms on the back of the chair in front of her, observing the room. Reed and Fergus are still leafing through old books. Flip has given up studying and is looking idly at old pictures of boxers on the wall. Evan is still sulking or raging. Bodi can't quite work him out yet. He seems nice enough but he does have a bit of a temper, then again with Balt as your dad it would be hard to keep a lid on it all the time.

Balt regains his composure. 'Take a break everyone. The teachers and I need a quick debrief to work out the best ways to make you a cohesive team. Given our time constraints we'll do the best we can to ensure you can work together and to your combined strengths.' They all go into the trainer's office and shut the door.

'Oooh! The drama!' Flip says to Bodi and they both laugh together for the first time.

The hint of smile on Reed's face as she walks towards him soon becomes a scowl when he sees she is headed past him to the changing rooms to find Evan. The changing room smells even punchier than the gym. Evan is pacing up and down, his fists clenched. It doesn't look like he's calmed down one bit.

'Evan? You okay?' she asks.

'Hey Bo. Sweet of you to check up on me. Yeah I'm okay I guess. Dad, well, you know…'

Bodi sits down on a bench and he sits with her. 'I'm really ready, really up for it. Ready to go get the baddies. My chi is aligned and all that.' He gives her a small chuckle but Bodi can tell he is struggling. 'This is what it's all been about, the years of training and the studying, but sometimes I don't feel I'm fighting my own fight.' He pauses, trying to contain what he wants to say but then it comes tumbling out. 'I feel like I'm always fighting his battles. All the time, every day. Where am I in this? Do I even get a say in what happens in my own life? It totally sucks.'

Bodi is surprised to see this side of him, she thought he was totally into it. She also lost her childhood but she hasn't been trained for anything, she hasn't been moulded in her mother's image against her will. She thinks about Ruby's decision to leave and raise her away from Populus. She is seeing first-hand what happens if you stay.

'He's quite formidable your dad,' she offers.

'You think?!' he laughs.

'What is it that he wants you to do?'

'Just stuff I don't believe in. Nothing specific.' Bodi knows he is covering something up but tries to coax more from him.

'It's not easy communicating with them at the best of times and this weird bubble we're trapped in doesn't make it any better,' she says. 'But I'm sure he wants what's best for you, deep down.

Whatever it is he's asking you to do…He's used to being a leader and he's gone into battle mode. Admittedly, he does look a bit like he's in that all the time…'

'No kidding,' Evan gestures at his soldier boy outfit.

'It's just clothes Ev. Maybe he even hides behind them so people can't see he's actually afraid. Well, maybe not afraid as such. He wears it as armour. But I can see that you're different and you aren't his little puppet. You've got your own style. Your own…' She stops. Thousands of pennies drop like a Las Vegas windfall.

'Boo?' Evan runs his fingers up and down the inside of her wrist. 'Boo? You alright?'

She pulls her arm away. It was Evan that she had bumped into at the park. And she gets the feeling he was there where she dropped her locket in the street. Populus had known she was coming to see them. For days. In fact, they had known she was coming even before she did.

'Erm, yeah, fine.' She almost whispers. She has to keep it together. She can't tell him what she is thinking.

'Am I in too deep now, relying on the one group of people that can't be trusted? Are they all Balthazar's puppets? What do they need from me?' she worries, but tries not to show it. She has to convince him nothing has changed. She still has to get her mum back. All this intrigue will have to be put on ice.

'There's no normal here Evan. But I'm sure we can make our own normal, eventually. I've got to believe that we can do it and you're a huge part of that. If you're not around, I don't think it's going to work.'

Ego suitably plumped, he smiles back at her.

'That's true Boo, we can't lose focus.' He jumps up on the bench and stands to attention. His softer side shut down once again. He offers her his hand to pull her up but she ignores the gesture. He pulls the front of his army sweater instead, jumps down and bundles out the changing room.

Bodi goes to follow him out of the changing room. 'Is Evan watching me? Are they all watching me?' she frets. The wheels are in motion and she won't be able to get off without doing herself, and her mum, some serious damage. She pushes the double doors and there is Reed pretending to be occupied in a book, but she knows he is waiting for her, for them, to work out what has gone down. She walks past him without acknowledging him. She can't deal with this dopey rivalry right now. And maybe he's in on it too.

Bodi joins the other three in the line of chairs. Flip is unhappy that Bodi and Evan had been having some alone time and sits with her arms and legs crossed staring straight ahead. Reed is eyeballing Evan, who sits to attention in his chair, ready for orders. Balt marches back into the room. 'If he could have a Sergeant Major's stick and rap us with it I'm sure he would,' thinks Bodi. 'Never mind Evan, this is the one that knows something that I don't and I need to find out what it is.'

'Thank you all for this morning. It's an unusual situation where we have to hand over the reins of an operation to our children but we hope that we have come up with a plan that will see the safe return of Ruby.' Bodi forces a smile for Balt. 'We have identified your skill set and together you make for quite a formidable team.'

Balt continues: 'We are working with our friends on the outside to implement a quick and safe plan to get Ruby back. The last thing we want is to put you in danger.

'So, I'm sure you're keen to hear, what the plan is. We are sending you out to infiltrate TrueSec HQ.' Balt holds up a photograph of a large, nondescript office building. 'This building is their central office in Charing Cross. We have different tasks for each of you to help us gather the information we need in order to get Ruby back in one piece.'

'Felicity. You are now the newest receptionist for TrueSec. A position I'm sure you will embrace with vigour. We need you to keep an eye on who is coming and going. But discreetly, of course. Hatty will fully brief you, go with her please.' Flip goes to high five everyone but is left hanging.

'At the other end of the spectrum. Boudicca, you will be joining the maintenance staff.'

'Maintenance? But I don't know one end of a spanner from another,' she says, bemused.

'Maintenance is a grand way of saying cleaner, Boo.' Evan tells her, smirking.

'This is where the real work happens Boudicca. You can get access to a number of high-level rooms and get near to restricted information. See documents before they're shredded, even unattended computers. We already have a couple of key operatives on the inside there.' Hatty and Morag exchange looks, Balt is getting a little carried away with the spy speak. 'Your first shift begins tomorrow at 6am sharp. Same goes for you Evan.'

Evan's face falls. 'Seriously?! A cleaner? That's the best you could do?' Bodi sniggers in retaliation.

'Unsurprisingly, as we are not whiter than white you'll stick out like a sore thumb doing anything *but* that around there. It is not what you would call a 'diverse environment.'

'And me? Am I on toilets or sorry should that be waste control management?' Reed's question drips in sarcasm.

'You, young man, have a bit of a challenge on your hands. I need you to resemble a junior clerk by 9am tomorrow morning. You are TrueSec's newest post room boy. Again, junior level jobs means you can move around the building relatively freely and unnoticed.'

Before Reed can complain, Bodi asks a question.

'How did you manage to get this sorted so quickly? I mean, all our paper work and contacting your inside men? Quite a feat in, like, *two* days.' She tries to sound neutral but her words come out with an edge of attack. Reed nudges her with his elbow. 'I mean, it's really impressive how you've got it together, thank you Balt.'

'Well, it's not been easy Boudicca but we are lucky in how we have kept our contacts close for many years now. One important fact, Ruby's prisoner number, it's B4579D. Bravo 4579 Delta. You all got that? That's what you've got to keep an eye out for.' Bodi repeated the number over in her head.

'You two, Boudicca and Evan, with me. Reed, you go with Morag and Fergus.' Morag brandishes a pair of hair cutting scissors between her index finger and thumb, snipping the air, relishing Reed's imminent short, back and sides. Reed leaves them begrudgingly.

'Who knew the key to a successful mission was vacuuming?' Bodi tries to make a joke but Evan just nods. He seems preoccupied again and so Bodi waits for Balt to come over to begin their training. Is he going to show them how to clean? She doesn't think so. He pulled up a chair.

'The key to successful information gathering...'

And so begins two long hours on what to look for in waste paper bins.

Bodi and Reed head back to Sam's, their minds numbed by talk of shredders and office layouts. She is pleased to see Sam's enduring smile and a huge pot of chilli on the stove. The birds are singing their evening chorus and the three of them sit down to a quiet meal.

'What a feast Sam. Thank you.' Bodi is genuinely moved.

They try to embrace their new routine and speak convivially for a while about the day: about Evan and Balt's fight, about the books Fergus showed Reed and how Flip had been insanely pleased with her assignment. It is like recounting tales after a long school day...but a weird version where the kids are going undercover in a high security company.

'So, honestly, how are you feeling about tomorrow? Ready for your day of glamour?!' Sam finds it hard not to point out the funny side of things.

'Sure. Can't wait to get those rubber gloves on. Essential spy kit.' Bodi tries to join in but just sounds flat.

'It will be fine. You'll be fine.' He rummages in his jacket. 'I need to give you your ID cards. I picked them up earlier from, well, you don't need to know that bit.'

Reed and Bodi take their cards from Sam. What should be a serious moment is broken by Reed's look of sheer disbelief. 'What? Is there something wrong with them?' Sam tries to grab the card back but Reed has passed it to Bodi, it reads "Maurice Applewhite".

'Maurice!' Bodi bursts out laughing. 'Maurice! Seriously?' It feels good to laugh. He adopts a super nerdy voice.

'Maurice Applewhite. I like train spotting and collecting glass ornaments and I'm 74 years old.' He checks out Bodi's ID 'Irena Kowalski. Cool spy name.'

'It was either Maurice or Kwame. I'm not sure you could've pulled off Kwame.' Sam said deadpan.

'Oh and one other thing.' Sam reaches under the table and pulls out a box which he places gently on the table in front of Bodi. It is black hair dye. The laughter stops as Bodi registers what it is. Reed looks aghast.

'We can't risk it Bodi. You're too distinct,' Sam says.

Bodi picks up the box from Sam and leaves the table. Back to feeling like her life is in someone else's hands again. It's getting increasingly more difficult for her to remember who she is.

Half an hour later, Bodi watches as her identity snakes down the drain as sludgy brown water. One more rinse and she will be Irena Kowalski. So much has happened since she was in this bathroom this morning. Bodi looks in the mirror that hangs over the sink. She doesn't even recognize herself so she guesses that is a good thing. She has managed to get the dye all round the edge of her face so she rubs at it with her shirt. She has never used dye before, in fact she is quite an amateur at anything to do with hair and makeup. She has been brought up to believe that she doesn't need it, and maybe Boudicca Jones doesn't, but Irena does. She wraps her shirt around her head and scrubs at her face a bit more. She has circles under her eyes and she looks paler than normal. Her rosy glow has faded to off white.

Lying on her bed is her work uniform: a blue nylon dress, some unremarkable trainers, some nasty tan tights and grubby white ankle socks. Bodi puts it all in a neat pile at the foot of the bed and adds a nub of an eyeliner pencil that Flip had given her earlier 'to help her look older'. She takes the Map of Inspiration out of her backpack and tacks it up on the wall beside her bed. If she is going to stay here for a few days then she wants to feel a little more at home. She stares at the scraps of faces and the faded quotes. It isn't giving her any answers today. Sam, or maybe Reed, has left a cup of warm milk with honey next to the bed and she sips it. She falls asleep. It is barely 10.

*R*uby reached up the bannister, stretching her leg out to cross the hole where the step should have been. Cal looked down the stairs at her, laughing.

'Oh yeah, we should really fix that,' he said with the hollow commitment of an alcoholic caretaker. 'Come on.' He grabbed her hand and pulled her the rest of the way up the stairs.

A mismatch of multi-coloured fabric hung like medieval pennants from the walls, pinned up with metal tacks. Most of them were patterned: gold tinged African batik tumbled over silk stripes running into swirling paisley. Some had slogans roughly hand painted on them in large black letters. 'I'm too young to be this ANGRY', 'Time to wake up' and 'We are the 99%'. Ruby ran her free hand along the walls feeling the fibres beneath her finger tips. The landing exploded in graffiti. An army of tiny pandas in tin hats were working together to attack a giant robot with mini cannons.

'This is where you live?' Ruby asked, trying not to sound too horrified.

'I'm staying with my brother for a while, and some of his friends,' Cal said proudly. 'Good, isn't it?'

Ruby swallowed her shock. This was not quite what she had imagined when Cal had asked her to come meet his family. That scenario had been terrifying enough and she had had minor palpitations deciding what to wear. Good job she hadn't gone with the 'I'm a nice girl really' dress and settled for some jeans and a stripy top. When he had met her by the tube Cal had greeted her with a 'you look nice?' clearly wondering why she would bother. And now she knew why. She doubted she would be making familial small talk about the weather over lasagne in this house.

'It's cool. Yeah.' She agreed though was at a loss as to what it was at all. Was it a squat?

He bundled her into a room which was suddenly bright after the hellish ascent of the stairway. The room had two disconnected old bathtubs sat in the middle of it, adrift like abandoned sail boats, they were piled high with books. The windows were bare except for some newspaper taped across it to keep out prying eyes. She followed him through this room and into a kitchen behind it. There she found a *bundle of people gathered around a kitchen table loaded with mugs and half-eaten packs of ginger biscuits.*

'The gallivanting young buck has returned!' a guy shouted from the stove. Then seeing Ruby apologised 'Oops! Sorry bruth.' Cal shrugged it off but it made Ruby wonder just how many girls Cal had brought back. The man rubbed his hands on a tea towel and walked over to her.

'Hello there...?' he looked at Cal enquiring about the name of their guest.

'Ruby', Cal said pointedly.

'Hello there Ruby. So pleased you could join us. I'm this reprobate's brother, Sam,' he smiled broadly and gestured round the room. 'And this is everybody. Everybody, say hello to Ruby.'

The motley assembled stopped their heated conversation momentarily to crow 'Hello Ruby'. She blushed and waved. She was not one to blush and normally had a lot to say, but this whole episode was entirely leftfield. She was mentally prepared for parental chit chat over a dining room table, not a squat of banners, books and bathtubs.

Cal sat on a chair and went to pull Ruby onto his lap. Mortified, she pulled away, sitting further round the table. Almost everyone around the table was around ten years older than her. She wanted to hold her own, not be the ditzy girlfriend. Cal scowled at her but she ignored him and tried to focus on what was being discussed. Cal rocked on the back legs of his chair and leaned into the fridge to grab two beers. He slid one along the table to Ruby who stopped it dead but left it unopened.

'All I'm saying is that that date won't work. There's too much police presence around the Cenotaph. Clement said we need to think round the problem a bit more. It's not Populus' style.'

'Well, if Clement says so. Maybe we should consider Marble Arch...'

Things were quite heated and Ruby wondered what they were discussing and who Clement was. He was clearly held in much reverence.

One of the men gave Ruby the once over, aware she was studying them. 'Maybe we should stop guys. You know...'

'You're fine Balt. I'm sure Ruby's heard all this before.' Sam said con-

spiratorially. 'Right Ruby?'

'Yeah. Don't stop on my account.' Ruby said, trying to look entirely clued up and retrieve her eyes from their stalks. Cal laughed knowingly, watching Ruby get sucked up into it.

'What's Populus? she asked naively.

THURSDAY

Fuelled by nervous energy, Bodi's internal alarm clock goes off around 4am and she lies staring at the ceiling. A few rogue birds are welcoming a sun that is far from up, making the smallest dent in the heavy silence. As she wakes she hears what she thinks is whale song, but it is a peculiar mix of police sirens and urban foxes calling to each other.

Yesterday flew by so quickly, Bodi can't imagine they are in anyway ready, but the more time they spend working on the plan the harder it will be to reach her Mum. She turns on the torch she uses as a night light. Shadows stretch their fingers up the walls. She puts the huge fur coat she is using as a blanket on her shoulders, steps into her boots on and heads downstairs.

Sam is already up. She spies a half-drunk bottle of whisky on the kitchen table and realises he hasn't been to bed. When she walks in he jumps. 'Jesus Christ! Going to take some getting used to, that look.' He slurs, waving his right hand in front of his face as if he is wiping the image of the new Bodi away. His head teeters on the knuckles of his left hand like it might come crashing down at any second. 'Ivanka?'

'Irena. Sam, seriously. Now? You choose *now* to pour yourself into a bottle?' Bodi goes over to the stove and puts the kettle on. 'I promised him. I promised Cal. 'Keep the boy out of it,' he says. 'Keep him away from them.' Sweet Cal, baby brother Cal. Always wanting to change the world to make it a better place but well, look where it got you, eh? That's him.' Sam waves a tiny snap shot at her. 'Us two before all this lunacy began. Before we started thinking we were the new bleedin' IRA. Brighton beach. Had a bit of money in our pockets and went off for the day on the train. Glorious.' His eyes fill with the tears of precious memories.

'Do you think it's time for bed Sam?' Bodi suggests, kindly.

'Don't wanna go to bed. Big day. Sending you all off...to jump off a cliff! Need to send you off properly.' He starts singing. 'Cheerio chin chin, pip pip, toodle oo, goodbyee!'

The kettle whistle blows. 'AttenSHUN!' Sam shouts, standing up and nearly tumbling to the floor. He steadies himself on the table and clinging to the furniture walks through to the library, collapses on the chair and passes out. Bodi turns the gas off, and drapes her fur coat over him. 'A lot of sadness under all that jollity,' she whispers.

Feeling the morning chill, she runs upstairs to grab a jumper. Reed comes lumbering out of his room.

'Whas goin on?' he slurs. Barely awake, and with no hair to hide behind, he looks particularly vulnerable. His eyes snap open at the sight of Bodi standing there in her underwear and boots. Her straight black hair drapes around her face making her eyes look bigger than normal and her pale skin even paler. She can't move and he can't stop looking at her.

She pulls at her hair 'It's the hair right? Can't quite believe it's me either.' She tries to sound amused but it comes across as melancholy.

'Oh yeah, the hair.' Reed says unconvincingly. He takes a step towards her and she doesn't move. He takes the strands of hair that she is holding from her and gives them a cursory glance. 'Just so different.' His eyes glance down but come back to her face. 'Your eyes.' He runs his fingers across her brow to push her hair away, avoiding her smarting eye. 'And your skin'. His eyes follow as his fingers move down to graze along her collarbone. She can smell his morning breathe and it isn't that hideous, more warm and sweet.

The two of them stand there, Reed's hand resting on the base of Bodi's neck, staring at each other, half in shock, half exhilarated. Her heart races, their breath mingling between them. They are inches apart, wrapped in the silence of the early day.

'You going to be okay today?' he asks so gently she can barely hear. She nods, looking at the floor.

'Who knows what today will be like if this is how it starts?' she wonders.

Reed lifts her chin up and looks her square in the eyes. 'It will be alright B. I'll make sure you're safe.' She smiles at him and he leans in and gives her the smallest, most tender kiss on the cheek and then goes back to his room.

* * *

Bodi meets Evan on the corner a block from TrueSec House. When she stands next to him he does a double take. 'Boo? Is that you? What the...?! I thought *I* looked different.' Evan has taken out his earring, removed his necklace and trimmed his hair but is still ostensibly himself. 'Mega vamp!' He laughs, making the sign of the cross with his fingers. 'Don't bite me! Actually, on second thoughts.' Bodi has drawn lines of kohl around her eyes and despite the uniform under her coat looks like she is a paid up fan of the dark side.

'We're very big on goth in Poland.' She tries out her Polish accent on Evan.

'Oh man, it is *way* too early for this. Cool, though. Very convincing.' She smiles appreciatively. 'But I miss my flame haired Boo. Hope she gets to come home soon.'

He pulls out a pair of round-framed glasses and puts them on. Hooking them over his ears he says, 'Meet Kwame Akoto.'

'So you got Kwame then.' She flashes her ID card at him. 'Hi Kwame, I'm Irena.'

'Irena and Kwame. The Polish goth and the Ghanaian nerd. Let's hope Reed doesn't need to do an accent, he's terrible at them.'

'You mean 'Maurice'.'

'Maurice! You're having a laugh. Seriously man. Maurice! Oh my days.'

Bodi feels a little disloyal talking about Reed like that, especially with Evan. The Evan that's been following her. She changes the subject. 'Time to go?'

Evan looks at his watch. 'Yeah it's six. You go Irena. I'll be right behind you. Our contact is Hardeep. See you on the other side.' He gives her a nudge in the direction of the staff entrance.

She doesn't know what to do with her fidgeting hands so shoves them in her coat pocket. Luckily it is fairly dark so no one can see she is agitated. She joins the queue at the staff entrance. The other staff give her a cursory look but they all have their own stuff going on. No one cares about yet another temp coming in to clean yet another office. Mostly the others are moaning about being cold and tired. The universal language of an early morning shift. Evan walks past and gives her the smallest wink, his head covered by the hood of his parka. Bodi looks up above her, this faceless tower is her Everest. To be conquered in record time.

The doors open and they start shuffling in. Regulars show their passes and go to pick up their cleaning equipment.

'New temps, this side.' A short man in a maroon turban indicates a desk behind him. His name badge says 'Hardeep'. Barely making eye contact Bodi nervously offers her ID card to him.

'Irena. Irena Kowalski.' Hardeep looks at her, nothing registers on his face.

'Wait in there please.' He points to a side room and she pushes open the door to find a table and some plastic chairs. Nothing to be scared of. She sits on one of the chairs, her hands still in her pockets. It doesn't feel like they have put the heating on in the offices. Probably doesn't come on until the 'real' workers clock in. She squints in the harsh strip lighting. She is momentarily lost in the sensation of Reed's kiss on her cheek and his hand on her collarbone.

A few minutes later Evan comes in. Swiftly followed by Hardeep, who shuts the door firmly behind him.

'We haven't got much time,' he says. 'In two seconds I'm going to take you to get your equipment and we're going to head to the

7th floor. This is where the most recent records are kept. They're written down before they're inputted into the computer system. You're going to have 30 minutes max before I have to move you onto another section. Plus you've got to try to do some cleaning in there or else my head will be on the block. Also security cameras. They will have a little malfunction in that area between 6.35 and 6.50 so that's basically your window. '

Bodi and Evan look at each other, a little startled but what choice do they have, they just have to go with it. They are in Hardeep's hands.

'Keep your coats on because the heating doesn't kick in until 8.30.' he raises his eyebrows. 'Plus, big pockets.' He does a double thumbs up. They both do it back, awkwardly.

'Where did Dad get this guy?!' Evan mouths at Bodi behind Hardeep's back, and they follow him out to pick up a vacuum and a box of cleaning supplies. Hardeep takes them to the service lift that has a heady smell of body odour and cheap bleach.

'The night guard's hygiene is a little suspect.' Hardeep offers by way of explanation. Other cleaners get into the lift with them, leaving in groups as they ascend the building. Bodi notes that they stick to their countries. Croats with Croats, Algerians together and so on. A small piece of home clung to in an otherwise unforgiving city.

She counts down the lights on the lift up to the seventh floor. They are the last in the lift. Hardeep points down the corridor. 'Room 709. Hope you find what you're looking for,' he says and the lift doors close. They are on their own.

Evan opens the door and turns the lights on, there are two desks facing each other in the middle of the room surrounded by floor to ceiling shelves crammed with files. Plus both desks have about four huge piles on them as well. Library ladders hang from rails in the ceiling. Bodi checks her watch, it is 6.25am. They have ten minutes to recce the room before the security cameras fail. While Evan plugs in the vacuum cleaner, Bodi sets about dusting. All the while they both have their eyes scanning the room. They note where the cameras are and move around the room slowly trying to work out if there is some kind of system in place. 'B4579D, B4579D.' Bodi repeats the number over and over in her head as the seconds tick down. Evan is speeding round with the vacuum and it drowns out any chance for talking about what they will do.

Despite being neat and uniform, the spines of the files don't have anything written on them. Bodi can't risk pulling them out while the cameras are still on so she looks for another clue. She bends down and looks at the shelves themselves. 'Are they marked with anything? Yes! Letters. The shelves are alphabetised.' Evan is trying to work out what files are on the desks, without actually moving or touching anything. It is hugely frustrating. Like crouching, waiting for a starting pistol that may never fire. Evan looks at his watch and at the cameras, there are red lights that will go off once the line is cut. Evan holds up two fingers. Two minutes. Bodi starts looking for the B shelf. She moves her duster along the edge of the shelves as she goes trying to look as bored as possible while the camera is still recording. She accounts for S, then R, then P. The system sweeps up round the room in a huge spiral. Bodi's eyes follow the spiral right up to the ceiling. If she is right then the B section will be at the top on the far wall. Balt told her that all she has to do is get the name of the facility and the arresting officer from the file. He said it should be on the first page. Should be… But she has to get that file first.

Bodi looks back to the camera and at that moment the red light goes out. She races across the room to grab the nearest ladder and move it round to where she thinks the file will be. Other files and books get in the way, it isn't the easiest of processes. "More haste less speed". The old saying jumps into her mind from nowhere.

'Breathe Boo. You need to breathe.' Evan tells her, helping to move boxes out of the way of the ladder and then put them back where they were. The office will have to look exactly how they found it.

Bodi stops and scampers up the ladder like a monkey while Evan is still moving it. 'It should be here.' She says, running her finger along the label on the shelf, the sticky tape has come unstuck and it is barely legible. 'That's C, back a bit.'

Evan pushes her round, moving and replacing files. This is not quick.

'Time check, five minutes down. Hey, cut it out Boo. You'll fall.'

Bodi is leaning off the ladder hanging by two fingers, trying to read the labels. The ladder catches up with her and she starts to pull out more files.

'You look on the desks Ev, she might not have been filed yet.' Adrenaline is pumping through them, her breathing quickening and getting louder. The door handle rattles and Evan grabs the vacuum and sticks it in the way of the opening door. A security guard tries to barge his way in. 'What are you doing? Let me in,' the guard shouts.

Bodi slides down the ladder and makes a grab for a cloth. 'Just cleaning mate, give me a minute,' Evan instinctively drops his Ghanaian accent for his London drawl. Bodi slides down the ladder, burning her hands, and grabs a cloth. Checking she is okay, Evan moves to let the guard in. 'What is happening here?' the guard asks. 'You're not meant to be in there.'

'It's fine mate. That bloke told us to clean in here,' Evan's accent is all over the place.

Bodi tries some Polish and a smile: 'Nie mówię po polsku.'

The guard looks at them suspiciously and reaches for his radio. Evan picks up the vacuum and with all his might hits him over the head with it.

'Ev! What the hell?! Are you crazy?' Bodi hisses at him. The guard is out for the count and his head is bleeding. Evan uses the vacuum's electric cable to tie him up. He grabs the cloth from Bodi's hands and shoves it in the guy's mouth.

'What the hell, Ev?! Now we're totally busted,' she panics.

'What did you say to him anyway?'

'Err…I told him I don't speak Polish. In Polish. Argh!'

'He was going to rat us out.' He reaches to the guard's neck to check his pulse. 'It's fine. What are you doing? Get on with it! We've got like two minutes left.' Evan shifts the guard out of the way of the cameras then leans his weight against the door.

'Okay, okay,' Bodi says, pulling out more files. 'No. No. Not that one. Come *on*.' Her agitation is tangible. She has file B4506A in her hand. 'That's more like it.' B4553C. She is nearly there. She nudges the ladder along the rail using her body weight; it creaks loudly and the guard groans. B4579B, two more, B4579C, B4579E. 'No D? What?' she checks again.

'It's not here. Ev, it's not here!' She checks either side, dismayed. She reaches over and behind the files to see if it has shifted back. Everything is in immaculate order. These clerks obviously do not misplace anything. 'Evan check the desks, they must be looking at it.' Evan looks at her and shakes his head. He is scanning the last pile and hasn't found it. 'Try again,' she begs.

'One minute Boo. One minute and the cameras are back on us. We've got to go! NOW!' Evan insists.

Like a petulant toddler being told to get down from a climbing frame, she climbs down the ladder begrudgingly. Evan hurries her along to the lift, hand in the small of her back.

Bodi repeatedly pushes the lift button sensing it won't be long until the guard wakes up. Evan is jigging from one foot to another like an agitated kid awaiting a treat. All the way down in the lift Bodi is waiting for an alarm to sound and she counts down the floors as they descend. The guard on the door lets them out after Evan mimes smoking a cigarette. Once the door is shut behind them they walk as quickly as they can to the nearest corner and once out of sight they run.

'I feel like it's the middle of the afternoon already. These early starts are a killer.' Evan says, trying to lighten the mood, but Bodi isn't listening. She feels worn out, physically and mentally. She really thought they would leave the offices with the information they needed to get on her mum. Time is flying by and she can't get the thought of her mum being tortured out of her mind.

The TrueSec alarm is wailing and despite being a few blocks

away now they could still be caught. He touches her arm and she shrugs him off. Evan is riding high on adrenaline. Bodi isn't sure his motives for hitting the guard were entirely justifiable. 'I'm sorry Boo. But these things can take time. And we've got Flip and Reed going in soon. Maybe they'll have better luck. If they can get in the building… Might have messed that one up a bit.'

Reed. She has forgotten all about him. 'I've got to go.' And she races off leaving Evan standing.

The bell tinkles over the door as she enters the café. She returns the greeting of the woman behind the counter and spots him at the far end of the room. His head down reading, he has drained his mug and is avoiding being moved on. She looks at him for a while, sat alone in the dark corner of this greasy spoon. She feels connected to him instinctively but on paper he is still a stranger to her.

'Hey,' she says. He scowls when he looks up, then beams when he realises it is her, not a black-haired stranger.

'Hey. How did it go?' he asks.

She slumps into the chair opposite him. 'Big fat zero. It wasn't there. Every other file was there but hers was missing. I don't know why. Oh and Evan punched out a guard, so…'

'Evan what?! Idiot. I bet we can't even get in now.'

She takes in Reed's new look. She is almost used to his short hair-cut, his white patch has almost disappeared, but he is wearing a Harrington jacket over a shirt and tie, suit trousers and black shiny shoes. And not one ring clutters his fingers. They are all actors in today's drama.

Aware she must be coming across like a sullen teen, she forces a smile and changes the subject: 'Ooh look at you. Well smart.'

Reed isn't buying it. 'B, I've got like two minutes so I'm just going to say this then I'm off.' He looks her in the eye and reaches his fingers across the table to touch the tops of hers. The knots in her stomach slacken a little. 'We are doing all we can to find your mum, in our peculiar, drawn out way. I know that Balt is like, highly suspect, but he has mobilized the troops on this one. There's a lot going on behind the scenes. You are going to have to keep believing that we can make this work otherwise it's going to be a struggle, for all of us. We want to help but you have to keep moving forward with us.'

'I am, I just…' Bodi feels bound by frustration.

Reed walks round to the back of her chair and puts his hands on her shoulders.

'I know.' He whispers in her ear and leaves. She feels both comforted and abandoned at the same time.

Back at the house she whistles at the birds who give her a welcome trill in return. She calls out for Sam from the kitchen but the house is empty. She wanders round different rooms: the kitchen, the library, her bedroom and finally Reed's room. She isn't sure what she is looking for specifically but she wants more answers. Her anger and fear have given way to a kind of numbness on the way back to the house. She cannot reconcile not having got any closer to finding Ruby.

She is drawn back to the photograph of her mum by Reed's window. 'Where are you?' she asks, looking in minute detail at the grainy image. Scanning the faces around the foot of the statue where she herself had sat just days ago. She recognizes Sam or is it Calder? Everyone else is pretty much a blur. A young man is on Sam's shoulders reaching out to Ruby. It might be Balt. Bodi isn't sure. Something else catches her eye, her mum is wearing the locket round her neck. Bodi instinctively reaches for it and it comes undone. Since she had prised it open it doesn't stay shut and the small piece of paper falls out into her lap. Bodi opens it, scouring the list for any further clues. There is one final address on there that she hadn't visited. Mainly because Sam has been so welcoming she hasn't felt the need to move on. Maybe this person knows more and could help. She checks her watch. She has three hours until she is meeting at the church for a 'debrief'. Bodi is amazed at how quickly she has taken to the military jargon of the group.

She changes out of her uniform, laying it neatly on the bed for the next day, then realises she won't be going back after today's fiasco. She touches the Map of Inspiration for good luck, hoping with all her heart that Reed and Flip are finding out things that she couldn't, and sets out to find out who this final friend of her mum's might be.

Forty minutes later she is standing in a very well to do area replete with immaculate stucco fronted houses in different pastel shades. Signs announcing "Guarded by TrueSec" sit proudly on each manicured lawn. Black armoured town cars sit outside the houses, shining with wax polish. Roses climb perfectly along trellises and bay trees in earthenware pots stand sentry duty either side of candy coloured front doors. Bodi sticks out like a sore thumb, even in her plain clothes. Bodi double checks the address. 'This is the right road,' she thinks, 'but why would mum know anyone who lives here?' This is as far from their lives as she can imagine. Perhaps the woman works at the house as a housekeeper? Bodi sits opposite the house for a while observing, working out her next step. If she speaks to the wrong person then she could mess things up even more.

The quiet is broken by the sound of a strained revving. Turning the corner is an electric golf cart carrying two paunchy TrueSec security guards. 'Clearly they aren't expecting any high-speed chases around here,' Bodi thinks, ducking behind the garden wall she is sitting on. They trundle past oblivious. Bodi waits a few minutes until they have turned into the next block and crosses the road towards the house, fixing her clothes as she goes to look as presentable as possible. She currently looks like a teenage cat burglar, a look that isn't going to instil confidence in anyone, be they the housekeeper or the lady of the house. She searches down the side of the house for a staff entrance but it is blocked by a heavy-duty gate topped with broken glass stuck in cement. So she goes to the front door praying that one of the staff answers.

She rings the bell, a giant lion's head with a bell button for a nose. She peers through the glass-panelled door but the frosting means she can't see much. When she hears the clip of expensive high-heeled footsteps, not the padded shoes of domestic help, she turns to leave. When the door opens and she can't help but look back. Her jaw drops. There, at the doorway, is a woman identical to her mother except she is wearing a pale pink silk blouse with a neat, wool pencil skirt. Pearls sit at her neck and on her ears. Her make-up is flawless down to the pale gloss on her lips and blush on her cheeks. Her auburn hair is pinned up in an immaculate chignon. It is like her mum but shinier. The woman looks straight at her with fear in her eyes, she hastily checks up and down the street.

'Inside! Get inside,' she commands in a loud whisper. Bodi keeps staring as she walks towards her.

'Mum..?' she asks, totally thrown.

'Shhh,' the doppelganger hurries her inside.

The room is sumptuously decorated with pale oyster silk on the walls, gilt-framed oil paintings sit under brass picture lights and huge swag curtains in cream linen shut out the outside. Crystal decanters and glasses sit on silver trays. The table is set for twelve, with fresh flowers bringing a small splash of colour into an otherwise sombre room. The room is filled with the opulent smell of freesias, brandy and furniture polish.

'You're not my mum right, cos that would be too weird...' Bodi stands behind a dining chair, gripping the back for support, she feels a little woozy. The woman stands stiffly opposite her; all the while her eyes darting towards the shut door anticipating unwanted company.

'You really can't be here Boudicca.' She stutters Bodi's name like it is the most complicated word she has ever had to utter. 'It is you? It's just with the hair and the make-up...'

'It's a long story. Normally I look more like you. Whoever you are...' Bodi keeps staring at this woman.

'Why on earth did your mum send you?' the woman asks aggressively.

'Who are you? Like her double or something?' Bodi is struggling to put two and two together.

'I suppose so. I'm Rose, your mother's twin sister.'

'You're my *aunt*?'

Rose lets slip a smile. 'Yes, I'm your Aunt Rose.' She walks over to Bodi and offers her hand to shake. Bodi just looks at it. Her mother's hand. But not.

'I have an aunt?' It isn't really sinking in. Rose nods.

'Where is Ruby, Boudicca? Is she in trouble?' Rose utters this as if she has said it many times in her life about her troublesome twin.

'The Sick Boys took her on Sunday. I'm trying to find her but it's impossible. I don't know what to do and Balthazar has all these plans and I don't know if they'll work. And it's been days and I couldn't find the file. Can you help me?' The words pour out of her like wine from an uncorked vat.

'Balthazar! You're involved in Populus? I thought Ruby was well away from those lunatics. You really need to leave the house Boudicca. If you get found here we'll all be in a world of trouble. I can't believe that she is back with them. Didn't she learn the first time?'

Bodi shackles rise, and she resists Rose pushing her out of the room.

'She wasn't. We weren't. It's just that when she was taken I had no one else to turn to. She left me a list of people to contact and well, you're the last name on the list.'

Rose's face flushes with anger.

'Well, that's just typical. She'd happily send you off to join that insidious cult and leave her own flesh and blood till last.'

'Looks like she got it right because you're hardly welcoming me with open arms.' Bodi looks at Rose's hand wrapped around her arm and Rose lets go. She softens.

'I am sorry Boudicca. I am, truly. It's just this is not a safe place for you to be. My husband is due home quite soon and, let's just say, he's quite big in security. If it got out that a member of Populus was here, and not only that one that I'm related to, then it could jeopardise everything.'

'So it's not that it's unsafe for me, rather it might upset your fancy life?' Bodi is fast getting the measure of her aunt.

'I wish I could help. I really do.' Rose seems genuine.

'Then help me Rose. Help me to find my mum.' Bodi takes Rose's hand and tries to channel her despair through that touch. Hoping her own feelings of anguish and fear will reach Rose's heart, if she has one. Rose caves.

'Meet me tomorrow morning. Away from here. By Eros, on Piccadilly.'

'Okay. Sure. But before then can you try to find out something? Anything about where mum is?' Bodi pleads.

They walk to the front door, Rose reaches up to touch Bodi's face. She flinches. 'So like her.' Her eyes glisten with tears.

'Like you too.' Bodi adds as she walks away.

Bodi is racing to St James's to meet Reed when all she wants to do is go back to Sam's curl up and sleep under the Map of Inspiration. She needs some way to connect to her mum because she has never felt so distant from her. Her mind is buffeted by all that has happened today, she is living a nightmare in broad daylight. She pounds along the streets at super human speed knowing that if she walks slower everything will catch up with her.

As the working day ends, the sea of people walking the streets part in her wake. She is running on empty, drained by days of conflicting information and revelations. She has never felt so far away from Ruby. Not just physically but she feels a chasm growing between them, full of secrets. Her thoughts are so jumbled that her brain has shut them down. She simply has to get to the next place and the next and the next, and at some point she will piece it all together. The wind is picking up and she feels it numb her face. It feels good, cleansing almost. She wishes it would whip inside her ears and blow everything clear of her mind. She breathes deeply. The walking is calming her. She is going to see Reed soon and that feels like a happy distraction though she isn't sure yet. Her experience of boys is so limited she doesn't know whether his is normal behaviour. She has heard that friendships form quickly under stress, but is this something more? She can't put her finger on why she feels so open to him. Is it just the security of Sam's house and how they have taken her in? Is it as simple as that? Or does he understand her, connect with her? Perhaps he is just reaching out to someone who has lived a similar life to him. Kindred spirits through circumstance, perhaps? Yet more unanswered questions to add to the growing pile.

Bodi catches a reflection of herself in shop window and it stops her in her tracks. She looks older than her years. Her clothes, hair and make-up have turned her into a whole other person. She feels like a stranger in her home city. Turning the corner to the church, she hopes that the others have had a more successful day than she has. Waiting for Reed, tiredness overcomes her she sits on the step and leans her head on the doorframe. As the rain starts to fall, she looks like the refugee she now is.

'What are you doing?' Reed wraps his hands round hers, waking her. 'You're freezing.' Reed takes his already sodden jacket off and covers her with it. She still isn't quite used to the fact that his face isn't hidden behind a curtain of hair. She can see in his face that she looks even worse than she feels. She runs her sleeve under her eyes, her make-up must have run all down her face. Reed opens the door and they stepped inside the church that feels even colder than outside and Reed, with his arm around her, guides her along his well-worn route. The tunnel is full of puddles and Bodi stumbles a few times. The ladder seems never-ending though it is barely a few feet up to the trap door. She heaves herself up with Reed helping her.

They walk into the vault together and everyone turns to welcome her but they look shocked. Bodi is wet through and shaking. Morag runs to wrap one of her biggest scarves around her and Sam carries her over to an electric heater. Hot tea and a couple of digestive biscuits appear and Bodi sits on the floor next to the heater as people fuss around her. Even in this weirdest of circumstances, it feels like the most familial set up. Holding Sam's hand she walks over to where Balt is sitting with Evan, Flip and Reed. She feels better now she has dried out and warmed up a bit.

'Don't mind me, just been a bit of a long day.' She tries to make light of it. She looks at her watch. '5.30? Is that all?'

'Boudicca, we're just having a quick debrief and then we'll work out next steps. Evan has already told me about the missing file which is most unfortunate. And the guard. Not such a clever move. Hardeep's one of our best men so I'm surprised he was misinformed. Felicity was just telling us about her day.'

'No doubt hugely informative,' Bodi sneers.

'That's enough Boudicca. Sit down.' Balt barks at her. She drags a chair over with her foot and sits sulking.

Reed starts talking. 'How about I tell you what I found?' Bodi shrugs. 'Well, knowing that the file is missing I set about trying to find out where it could've got to, what the different options were. It started out slow, much like Flip I was trying to get the lay of the land. The post room staff has huge grudges but they're careful who they talk too, especially me. Why would they trust some newbie?'

'So basically we got nowhere.' Bodi grumbles. 'We're no closer to bringing my mum home.' She sounds flat. No tears, no emotion, just flat.

'Not quite. I saw that some new prisoner files, just a couple a day, get couriered to another building. I offered to do the run but they said no. Maybe if we can follow that courier we'd be one step closer to finding Ruby. It leaves at the same time every day so it would be fairly easy to do.'

'Good work Reed.' Balt says encouragingly. 'Very good. Let's talk logistics and we'll set up a team to follow this guy and take it from there.'

'In the meantime who knows where she is. But hey, well done team! Woo!' Bodi's sarcasm cuts the talk dead.

Sam steps in before Balt can let rip on at her about the strategic long game. 'I'm going to get this one out of here. Think she needs some alone time. Reed. Let's go.' Bodi happily extricates herself from the debrief. It is all mumbo jumbo to her anyway. She has her own ways to get her mum back.

'Bodi, we're just trying to help you but we're new to this too. Take it easy.' Reed is hurt by her lashing out.

'Why did I come here? Nothing is working. I might as well move on. I mean, what good are you to me?' Reed doesn't look at her any more, just guides her along the passage. She can tell he is fuming but Bodi doesn't care. They have let her down. She doesn't need them.

Sam bundles her onto the bus. She can't remember how they got to the bus stop. Another tunnel through another nameless building. There is a dull murmur of talking for a while but she hasn't really noticed. The bus is reassuringly warm and noisy so she doesn't have to listen to anything. The bus is an extravagance she isn't used to. She leans on Sam. Reed had stomped off at the earliest opportunity, leaving them standing at the bus stop. 'Teenagers.' Sam mutters under his breath.

Bodi and Sam alight after twenty minutes and walk the short distance to the house. Sam walks her straight up to her room telling Reed to wait downstairs. He puts her to bed.

'What's this then?' Sam gestures at the map.

'Inspiration.' She just about gets that out and nothing more.

'Always was one for hero worship your mum. Nelson Mandela, eh? Well guess that's fairly obvious. Who's that, Indira Ghandi? Bowie?'

'Red hair.' She mumbles into the pillow.

Every time she breathes in it feels like she is force-feeding herself air. There is nowhere for it to go. She wheezes as she breathes out, holding her hands to her throat to try to strangulate the coughing. If she wants to say something, she gulps in air, thinks what she has to say and spits out the words like grit.

Sam puts his head on her forehead. 'You're burning up. I'll go get one of my magic potions. Just stay there.'

Bodi looks up at him, with sad eyes. 'Not going anywhere, believe me.'

Bodi's fever has her shivering and reaching for blankets. The room is moving in and out on her with every heartbeat. She chastises herself to be well. Terrible timing. What about tomorrow, her meeting with Rose? She has to be there for that. By the time Sam returns with some hot nasty liquid in an old mug, Bodi's teeth are chattering.

'I thought you came back this afternoon for a rest? You're worn out.' Sam is squinting at her. He seems enormous to her and she feels like she has shrunk to the size of a mouse cowering in the corner of the bed.

'Couldn't sleep' is all she can manage.

'Fair do's. Drink this and then off you go, you'll feel much better in the morning. I've banished boy wonder. You don't need him moping about. I'll check in on you in a few hours but I think after this little draught you'll be out for the count. Might have a swig myself! Could do with a good night's sleep.' Sam gives the mug a big sniff. 'Huughwee, that's good.'

Bodi thinks it smells vile but chugs it down regardless. She is willing to try anything to be better by tomorrow. It tastes of old leaves and mustard. She just about keeps it down. Within seconds she is boiling hot and throwing off the bedcovers. This is going to be a long night.

She drifts off into a world of nightmares: whirling numbers and letters. Never ending corridors of files and books and infinite ladders that she can't be free of. Reed's face switching with Evan's, leaving her hanging by her fingers on the ladders, the floor miles below her. Evan laughing at her distress, challenging her to leap. Out of reach Ruby and Rose walk off together. They don't acknowledge her screams.

Bodi wakes at 11pm. She feels clammy all over, even her teeth ache. It takes all her strength to make it to the bathroom. The coolness of the bathroom floor is very welcome to the soles of her feet. She leans on the basin and looks at her reflection. The fever makes her sense of self even more remote. Her eyes are sunk in her head and the black hair doesn't help. It is sticking up everywhere like a witch after a bad spell. She crawls back to bed and pulls the covers over her head.

R uby crept into her room, dropped her backpack by the door and turned the light on.

'Where have you been?! Mother's verging on apocalyptic.' Rose fired at her as soon as she walked through the door. She was spread eagled on her sister's bed.

'Out. And what are you doing in my room?' Ruby whispered, trying to change the subject. Rose was wearing pink polka dot pyjamas with an R embroidered on the pocket. Her hair was tied up in a pink scrunchie. Her toe nails sparkled with iridescent polish. She was the prim to Ruby's improper.

'I was looking for my locket and I got distracted. And anyway, I'm not her. You can tell me, Reuben. Is everything okay?' Rose asked, concerned.

'You're the younger sister Rosebud, aren't I supposed to take care of you?' Ruby replied.

'By nine minutes. Honestly, are you ever going to let that go? So who is he? I know there's a boy.' Rose's eyes lit up with the possibility.

'There goes that twintuition again, sis. Have you been getting a feeling in your hoohah that there's romance in the air?!' Ruby cackled and flopped down in a chair, kicking off her high tops.

'URGH. Twintuition's a real thing. I know when something's up with you, Rouble. Just because you don't feel it doesn't mean it's not real. Like the time you fell…'

'Fell off the wall. I know. You 'sensed' it. Shame it wasn't your arm that got busted though, eh? It was sooo painful. You're sweet, Rosamundo, but seriously, it's a load of crap. Nice of you to worry about me. But I can take care of myself.' Ruby loved how they're so different. Rose was always going to tow the line and Ruby, well, she would yank the line from under her, turn it into a lasso and rein in trouble. Ruby shoved Rose off her bed, and she landed on the floor with a hard thud.

'Ow!' Rose wailed. 'What was that for?! Seriously, you're certifiable.'

'Just, cos I can. You're too trusting Rose, you need to toughen up a bit. People will always take advantage if you don't.' Rose threw a hairbrush at her sister and missed.

'Great shot!' Ruby mocked.

'ARGH you're SO annoying!' Rose stood up and went to leave the *room.*

'He's hella hot...' Ruby offered an olive branch. 'Oh my days. I die...'
She feigned passing out.

'Have you got a picture?' Rose rifled through Ruby's bag but Rose
waved her phone from across the room. She scrolled down to find the
only photo she has of Cal. He was not one for selfies.

'Hm. Way cool. Who are they?' Rose asked, pointing at the other
people in the background.

'His friends. They're cool too. Bit different. Got things to say, you
know?'

'About what?'

'Life. What's important. How to change things. It's challenging.'

'Ooh very deep,' Rose mocked.

'Not for the likes of you, goody two shoes. Mother would have a hissy
fit if she knew who they are. Very 'unacceptable'.' They both raised
their eyebrows. Rose kept the home fires under control while Ruby
ran riot. It had always been thus.

"That is unacceptable behaviour from a young lady," they chimed
together.

'Well, I had a very exciting day at school,' Rose said sarcastically.
'Double Maths. School? Remember that? Big brick building. Bursting
with hideous toffee-nosed bitches in hanging green uniforms. Run
by the most miserable women ever to walk the earth. Ring any bells?'

'Not really. Thanks for covering for me. I know it's a pain. Buts I loves
you for it.' Ruby squeezed Rose's cheek. 'I'm learning so much more
out there Rose. I. R. L.'

Rose rolled her eyes, 'You're unbearable! All free and no school and
boyfriends. I don't think we can be sisters anymore. I divorce you.
I divorce you. I divorce you. Or whatever the sisterly equivalent is.
I hereby un-sister you for having a life. Now I'm going to return to
mine. Good night.'

Ruby wished she could tell her sister that she loved her but they were
just not that kind of family. 'I love you' was as rare as 'My house, my
rules' was common. So she blew her a kiss but Rose had already left
the room.

FRIDAY

Sun streams in through the gaps in the curtains and Bodi reaches for the glass that she hopes Sam has put there. She finds some watered down orange juice and some paracetamol. She swallows them, gagging because they feel like razor blades sluicing down her throat. She drags herself to the bathroom again and tries to wash. She has an hour to get to Piccadilly to meet Rose and nothing is going to stop her. She creeps around, not wishing to disturb Sam or Reed. She rummages in her bag for her one nice item of clothing. A floral blouse that she inherited from her mum. She needs to feel like herself again. The pale blue helps to lift her face a little. She stifles the sound of her cough with a jumper. Bodi treads carefully on the stairs, clinging to the banister for support. A huge creaking step should alert them to her exit, but the house makes lots of noises and the birds' incessant chirping helps to cover her escape. She makes it out the gates though the floor feels like sand and she has to concentrate hard to make it to the road. Every so often she leans against a low wall or tree. There is nothing else for it; she is going to have to use her emergency funds to take the bus.

London trundles by her as she sits at the back of the bus, leaning her forehead against the window. What were once landmark buildings stand as shells; a fake movie skyline, a broken landscape. The city is in ill repair but it never stops. Nothing in history has been big enough to topple it entirely.

Bodi comes round as the bus approaches Piccadilly. A few advertising lights still shine powered by some unaccounted for electricity. Random letters jump out every so often from slogans for products Bodi has never even heard of. But the hazy autumn sun gives everything a warm glow. She feels like she is in the beating heart of the London, where once people congregated with friends and loved ones to take in the wonders of a much-loved city. Now it is a thoroughfare. Wooden boards wrap round the statue of Eros. It has been like that as long as she can remember. The top of the bow is just visible above the boards, his arrow always ready to strike. He has been caged like that since the riots and no one has thought to set him free since. Bodi leans on the hoarding hoping Rose gets there soon. People don't loiter here. Her knees crumple beneath her.

'Boudicca? Are you unwell? Can you stand?' Rose gets hold of her under one arm and picks her up and walks with her to a waiting 4x4. Bodi stumbles along, trying to hold her head up. Sweat drips from her forehead and she reaches out to steady herself on the side of the huge black car. Her eyes shut, she senses being picked up by someone much larger than Rose and laid down on a leather seat. Hushed, stern words are exchanged and the car starts to move.

Bodi wakes up in a small room with a tiny window high up above her. Around her is very basic furniture but it is extremely clean. She is in a proper bed with sheets and blankets and the floor is covered in linoleum with the pattern scrubbed bare. There is an old electric heater in one corner, no books, no radio. A small wind up clock ticks by the bedside, Bodi squints to read its face. Lunchtime. A packet of flu tablets lies half empty next to it. She must have taken some when she arrived, she can't recall. A photograph of two small children in a wooden frame sits on the nightstand, their faces set in unnaturally stern poses. A school picture perhaps. At the other side of the room the wall is lined with cleaning products. The smell of bleach and damp intermingle with the smell of cooking wafting in below the door. Roast chicken perhaps, but with something else added, it is an unfamiliar smell. Bodi's tummy rumbles. Thinking back she recalls being in her aunt's house, but is that today or yesterday? Everything is all jumbled up. How long has she been here? She makes her way to the door, which is locked. She treads on a note lying at the foot of the door. Pale pink embossed paper, unfolded it reveals a short note is written with a blue fountain pen: 'Boudicca. You are in our housekeeper's room. Please be extremely quiet. She will be in with some food when you wake. Rose.'

Bodi strains her ear at the door and hears piano music coming from somewhere. She climbs on the bed to look out the window which is sealed shut, but all she can see is a wall. She sits on the bed wishing she were back at Sam's. It might not be quite so clean there but at least she has the freedom to come and go as she pleases. And Reed is there. She tries the door again but nothing. Bodi sits back on the bed and waits. She wonders how Evan, Reed and Flip had got on today, whether they have found out where Ruby is being held. Sometimes it feels like seconds since she was home alone with her mum and sometimes it feels like months have passed. From one thought to another she swings from deepest despair to blind optimism. Her Mum is dead, Rose might have found her, Reed will never talk to her again, Balt might have a new source, Sam will never trust her again, soon she will be home with her friends. And so it goes until she hears the key turn in the lock and a small lady walks in carrying a tray. She wears a plain blue dress, a white apron and white trainers. Not dissimilar to what Bodi wore as Ivana. She puts the tray down and locks the door behind her, an action that looks habitual.

'I'm sorry, I think I have your bed,' is all Boudicca can think to say. The lady shakes her head.

'It's okay.'

'What is your name? Er *Tuhada naan ki hai?*' Bodi tries her Punjabi. The housekeeper is suprised and somewhat amused.

'Jasmeet.'

'Hi Jasmeet, my name is Bodi. Thanks for the food. Is Rose coming to see me soon? I need to leave.' She has to get out of there.

'Rose is with Mr Thomas,' she points upwards and puts her finger across her lips.

'Thank you Jasmeet.' Bodi whispers.

'She will come here later, when he leaves.' Jasmeet doesn't seem all that enamoured with 'Mr Thomas'.

'How long will that be?' Bodi wonders. Hours to pass and nothing to occupy her but her bad thoughts and her restlessness. She eats the soup, biscuits and fruit on the tray. She puts the rest of the flu tablets in her pocket. Bodi notices there is nothing breakable or sharp on the tray. Does Rose fear for Bodi's safety or her own? Is she being held prisoner? Her mind races with ridiculous scenarios where she will never leave this room again and where Ruby is never found. They are both locked up now and what good is that doing? Bodi stops and breathes slowly, trying to calm herself. She just has to wait and when Rose arrives she has to get out. It is as simple as that. She sits and listens to the second hand tick round the clock, like a dysfunctional metronome jarring with the piano music coming from above her.

Bodi stands up sharply ready to bolt when Rose finally comes in, an hour later. Again, it is like looking at a sanitised version of her mother and she leaves the door open, both of which throw Bodi.

'How are you feeling?' Rose goes to feel Bodi's forehead but Bodi steps away from her. Rose's breath smells of wine and cigarettes.

'I need to go,' Bodi insists.

'Right, well, that's your prerogative.' Rose steps to one side.

Confused, Bodi goes to leave. 'Just like that?'

'Sure. You can stay. If you'd like. Jasmeet can sleep in the garage. She has a bed roll.'

'A bed roll? In the garage?' Bodi's tone barely contains her disgust.

'I hardly think it's your place to comment on my staffing arrangements Boudicca. And it gives her money, to send to her family.'

'I must've missed the lesson on managing a mansion.'

'To be fair, your mother had enough experience to teach you all about that.'

Rose's bitterness is met with shock from Bodi. 'What do you mean?'

'Never mind. That was a long time ago. Are you well enough? Arthur can take you where you want to go. Our driver. From earlier?'

'I must go, people will be worried.' She hesitates. 'Thank you, Aunt Rose, for bringing me into your home. Well as much as you could. I realise it's very difficult for you to have me here.' She walks past Rose who pointed her towards the back door. 'Before I go, do you know anything else about Mum?' Rose smiles taking another piece of pink writing paper from her pocket and hands it to Bodi.

'I really do hope Ruby's okay. Please tell her I think of her every day.'

Bodi hears Rose sniff back tears as she walks away.

Half an hour later she walks in the door of Sam's house to find Balt sat with Sam at the kitchen table. They both stand up with a jolt. Balt looks down at her sternly, 'Where on earth have you been, young lady?' Sam rushes over to her and gives her a huge hug. 'Pop down the shops, did you? Forget your key?' She hears footsteps race down the stairs. Reed. And Evan.

'Are you okay?' they both say it together and stop, glare at each other. Bodi manages a smile. It is nice to be back in the mad house. She hands over Rose's note to Balt. He opens it and reads aloud 'Kenwood House'. He passes it to Sam. 'How did you get this?'

Reluctantly she answers them. 'Rose.'

'Rose! You got it from Rose! How did you even...' Bodi can see the rage in Balt's eyes. 'Do you even know? Do you understand what danger you've put us all in?'

'Balt, seriously man, less of the drama.' Sam intervenes.

'Who's Rose?' Evan asks.

'My mum's twin sister.' Bodi says.

'Yes, Rose is Ruby's sister, but she is also Mrs Thomas Cleaver.' Balt is fuming.

'The head of TrueSec, Thomas Cleaver? Wow. Way to go Boo, straight to the top!' Evan looks impressed. Balt scowls at him.

'Well, it's better than emptying bins for scraps of paper, Pops.'

'How did you even know about Rose? I thought she and Ruby hadn't talked for years.' Sam asked.

'I didn't know she existed until yesterday. Mum left me a note. You were on it, some other people from Populus. She was the only one I hadn't contacted, so I went to see if she could help and well, it turned out she could. I didn't know we were related. I've never met any of my relatives.'

Balt looks at his watch. 'How did you get back here? Did they bring you?'

'I got them to drop me like six streets away. I wouldn't endanger you Sam.'

'That's my girl!' he says proudly.

Balthazar turns to Sam and flares up again. 'You have to move Sam. You'll be the first one, then we'll all get taken down. You know how you are under pressure, your mouth just shoots off to save your ass-'

'I cannot believe you'd bring that up, it was twenty goddamn years ago...' And they are off, squabbling like old ladies over who should pay for tea.

Reed has remained quiet through all this, watching and listening. He extracts Bodi from the melee, draws her into the library and sits in an armchair, pulling her onto the arm.

'I thought you'd left. You were so sick, I thought you'd fallen down in the street and been hurt. You didn't leave a note,' his voice breaks slightly with controlled anger.

'I had to go Reed. I can't explain it. I had a feeling that she'd come through for me. I had no choice.'

Evan walks in the room and Bodi automatically stands up. Reed reaches for her hand but she shrugs him off. Wounded, he retreats back upstairs. The adrenaline is wearing off and she is sick of talking. Evan sits down in the other chair, keeping an eye on her while she contemplates the day so far. Balt and Sam are still hammering away at what they will do with this new information. Bodi feels a little reassured by the closeness of the books and the dim light.

'So, you've got an aunty.' Evan breaks the silence.

'Yeah, weird right? I'm so used to having no family, I was pleased to meet her but then she is who she is…'

'Bitter sweet.'

'She looked just like my mum but so different. Freaked me out.'

'I get it. Like invasion of the body snatchers!'

She laughs. 'Where's your mum Ev?'

'She left when I was about 5. She was never that into Populus. Her and Dad had been together since school you know but he got all political and she wanted a quieter life. She stuck it out for so long and then she found someone else, someone she could have a more normal life with. The guy didn't want me around. So here I am. I've got a whole heap of cousins and that, but we don't see them. So Populus is our family. Well, that's how dad sees it. God help me.' Evan gestures next door and rolls his eyes.

'But when do you get to leave? When do we all get to come out of hiding? Why do we have to pay the price of our parents' crazy ideas our whole lives?'

'Sometime soon I'm thinking I can go off on my own, start again somewhere new. But if I don't have him, who do I have?'

'I guess.'

Bodi takes this moment of quiet chat to bring up what has been bothering her since the gym. She asks quietly and without confrontation. She doesn't feel angry anymore, more intrigued.

'Why were you following me? Before, in the park, on Westminster Bridge? How did you even know where I was? Or who I was?'

Evan turns to her shocked, then laughs.

'Busted! D minus in spy school for Evan.'

'Ev! Come on.' She punches his arm.

'I didn't know who you were. Dad got me doing it. Said it was 'real world' training. Gave me your address, told me to keep an eye on you for a few days and report back. When you walked into the bank the other day I was gobsmacked. Had to front it out though, you know, cos you didn't recognise me I guessed I'd done a stand up job.'

'So you saw them take mum away as well?'

'Yeah, and I really wanted to help her, but I'd been told not to intervene in anything, just report back to dad. I had no clue that your mum was who she was. One of us. And well, you...I didn't know you then. I'm sorry Boo. I would've helped if I'd known.'

Bodi sits there thinking. So Balt is the only one who knew where they were living. None of the other Populus members knew she was coming. Evan is obviously clueless. Obedient, but not in on the wider plan. But how to get information from Balt when she needs to keep him on side?

She heads upstairs, stopping briefly at Reed's door. That will have to wait too. In her room the Map has come unstuck at one corner, so she pushes it back up. Her eyes fall on words she knows by heart. A verse by Maya Angelou, her mum's favourite poem.

The caged bird sings
with a fearful trill
of things unknown
but longed for still
and his tune is heard
on the distant hill
for the caged bird
sings of freedom.

And she chants her daily mantra, 'I'm coming Mum. Hold on.'

* * *

The men make for a ramshackle bunch around the kitchen table. Bodi sees that Sam has made a loaf of bread, which she knows from experience is barely edible, but toast it and slather it in butter and it just about does the trick. Pots of tea and piles of mismatched cutlery make for a very homely scene. Sam is playing Jimi Hendrix on an old cassette deck. It has clearly had a few hundred plays and warps every so often. Any sense of foreboding has dissipated temporarily. It is like any regular family meal: squabbling over food, washing up piled in the sink, the teenage boys grunting responses to their exasperated elders.

Bodi drinks it in. It is a scene she has imagined so many times in her head. What it would be like to have a bigger family, have siblings, a father who was around? In their very different ways they all contribute to a new sense of security for Bodi and she feels a little more human than she has in days. Is this her family now, or when she gets Ruby back will they have to move on again? Right at this very moment she is torn, she would find it hard to leave. She pulls a chair in between Reed and Evan and smiles at each of them in turn. They bathe in her attention and beam back at her like expectant puppy dogs anticipating a treat.

'The princess graces us with her presence!' Sam declares and nudges the toast toward her. 'Nice crown.'

Bodi's hair is wrapped in a royal wedding commemorative tea towel. The top of the golden crest haphazardly placed like a wonky tiara. She has used up the last of her shampoo to get rid of the dye in her hair. Her scalp is burning red hot but it is worth it. She pulls the towel off and lets her red curls fall down her back.

'Our Icenian queen returns. Hallelujah!' Sam exclaims. 'Ivanka the Pole be damned. It's good to have you back Boudicca.' He ruffles Reed's crew cut. 'Now if this one stays as he is we can have an Emo-free household.'

Everyone waits for a sharp retort from Reed but he just laughs along with Sam. His eyes shine. He no longer needs his hair to hide behind. Bodi hooks her foot round his under the table, keen to show him she is sorry. She wants to keep this, whatever it is, under wraps for now. It is just for them and Reed understands. Reed nudges his elbow closer to hers. Not so anyone notices but they know; they are in this together from now on.

'Sorry to break up this happy scene.' Balt sounds far from apologetic, rising above the table blocking the light. 'But we've got to get things moving again.' They turn off the old tape player and clear the table ready to discuss the plans for the rest of the day. All the while Bodi watches Balt, trying to work out what is going on behind the scenes. His face shows nothing of what his true plans are.

'I've heard back from my sources at Kenwood and it appears that we have conflicting information. They can't confirm that Ruby is being held there.' Bodi wonders how on earth he has achieved that in two short hours. Does he just make this stuff up?

'What do your 'sources' say then?' Bodi asks.

'Just that. But what we found out while you were off playing lone detective is that Ruby is being held in Richmond.'

Bodi shivers, feeling her mum move one more step away from her.

'Sam and I have come up with the bare bones of a plan for getting Ruby home. We need to talk to the other members of Populus. Morag and Fergus know a lot about the layout of Richmond and Mo has other contacts there. I know you probably expected a finalised action plan but it's one of the most secure buildings in the city. We would normally spend weeks planning an attack.' Balt corrects himself. 'A 'break out' rather, like this. We are meeting shortly at the bank to put our plan to them and get their informed input. We have decided that it will be a closed meeting for original Populus members only. Information that feeds into this, on our past dealings with the S.I.C., has to remain restricted.'

Reed speaks up. 'We know what you did Balt. It's well documented. I don't think you can pull anything out of the bag now that we don't already know about.'

Balt looks at him witheringly. 'I wish that were the case Reed, but as much as we can, we try to protect you from certain things. It may just be parental wishful thinking, but I ask you to humour us on this.'

'But what about Kenwood? I can't see why Rose would give me false information. She's better connected than anyone. We can't just ignore it.' Bodi is antsy, drumming her fingers on the table. She feels well again and wants to get moving. Another redundant day looms for them and Balt is putting more barriers between her and Ruby.

'But we saw sight of the file and my sources confirmed it, Boudicca. You just need to leave it with us for a few hours,' Balt is not playing ball. And when did he see the file? That's news to Bodi.

'And what are we meant to do in the meantime? Go out to play?' Evan says, just as unhappy being kept out of things.

'I'm sure you can find something to occupy yourselves Evan. Think of it as a rare evening off. There is one fact that I should make clear from the outset - and on this Sam and I are in agreement - Boudicca, you will not be involved in executing the plan.'

'You have got to be kidding!' Evan expresses Bodi's dismay for her.

'Your little mission to see Rose nearly cost us the whole organization. You put Sam in danger, and Reed. I don't think you're quite aware of the impact of your actions. If you can't work with us, then I can't include you in this. We will get Ruby back for you but you will not go near Kenwood House.'

'But the reason we know where they're holding mum is *because* I went to Rose,' Bodi protests.

'But that information isn't legitimate. We have to put a bit more time into this to get it right. Operations like this put a lot of people in plain sight, the exposure can have an irrevocable impact. We have been on top of things from the outset but a wrong move now could cost us everything.'

'Yeah right. You were really on top of things. Don't make me laugh. You had us clearing out bins and stalking postmen. Hardly the CIA!' she scoffs.

Balt sighs, exasperated by her. He puts his hand in her face to say, it's done, you can't undo it now.

'Sorry duckie, but I'm more concerned about the authorities getting to you,' Sam says kindly. 'I couldn't bear to not have you around anymore. Best to keep you safe here.' He tries to appease her with a reassuring smile but Bodi freezes him out.

'Bodi. We're on your side.' Bodi is surprised to hear that from Reed. She looks at him, hurt. 'I mean, if it keeps you safe.'

'You cannot control me Balt. I am not your daughter. I am not part of Populus. Your rules don't apply to me. I didn't even know you people until less than a week ago and now you're telling me what I can and can't do. It's *my* mum we're talking about.'

'And you compromised your involvement in this mission the moment you went to Rose,' Balt sneers.

'Mission? Oh my god. You are not an army general Balt. You are a group of crusty misfits in hiding for things you did a million years ago. You aren't relevant anymore. No one is scared of you. You don't mean anything to anyone!' Bodi is fuming. 'And just for the record, I didn't know who Rose was. For all I knew she was just another Populus nut job like you lot. I wasn't trying to hurt anyone but honestly, what was I meant to do? Ignore the fact that she could save us days and days of searching and getting nowhere?'

'Well it was this group of 'nut jobs' that has kept you fed all these years, we 'crusty misfits' have kept a roof over your head. How do you think that Ruby looked after you? Money doesn't come out of thin air you know!' Balt counters.

'I never asked for it. Mum kept me away from you for a reason. She knew what mental cases you were. Sad mental cases playing soldiers.' Bodi is almost screaming. Her face is beetroot with frustration. She can't help feeling like she is being treated like a hysterical little girl.

Sam stands up. 'That is enough Boudicca. I understand that you're angry but please don't reduce us to such banal stereotypes. We are trying to help you as best we can. We are your friends, and though you might not believe it right now, we are your best hope of bringing Ruby home.'

Bodi touches Sam's arm. 'Well that scares me Sam. And I'm sorry. I don't mean to be rude to you after you've been so kind to me. But I feel like we're wading through quicksand. Mum is getting further away and having to sit home in my princess tower so the baddies don't get me! I just won't do it!'

Balt gets up to leave. 'We will not waver on this Boudicca. That is my final word.'

Boudicca goes to lay into Balt again but Evan takes her hand and drags her out of the room. 'When he's like this it's not worth fighting him. Believe me. And you know maybe he's got a point. Not about the Rose stuff but about keeping you away from danger.'

Bodi takes a step back, shocked. 'You too?!'

She is surrounded on all sides by men that want to control her. She goes up to her room and slams the door like a punished child. She sits on her bed, absentmindedly twisting a blanket round and round with her hand, trying to work out what her next move should be. She is certain she can do something without the help of Balt and his minions. She hears the back door shut as Sam and Balt leave for their secret powwow.

'What do they know about me or Mum even? Their idea of her is of how she was. She's so different now,' she thinks. A sadness sweeps over her. 'Is this my life now? With them telling me what to do? And the nerve of them, keeping me out of everything like a precious doll. I've never been that and if they knew me-' A sharp knock at the door disturbs her inner ranting.

'What?!' she snaps.

'Erm hi Bodi.' Bodi is surprised to see Flip's face poke round the door. 'I can go away if you want. Probably best, eh?'

'Come in Flip. Sorry, thought it was one of *them*.'

Flip gives her room the once over.

'I like what you've done with the place.'

Bodi laughs.

'And those birds, honestly, they totally creep me the hell out. Why would you even do that?' She visibly shivers.

Bodi clears some stuff off the bed and Flip sits down next to her. She looks as though she had been invited to sit on a muddy log.

'So what are you doing here? Did they panic and send for female reinforcements?' Bodi asks.

'Pretty much. They all stress a bit about 'girl stuff'. Think that they've managed to tune themselves out of dealing with women. That side of their brain has almost shut down from lack of use. Or it was never there to begin with.'

'It's just so prehistoric. Don't you think?'

'I wouldn't say that it's entirely sexist. It's more like Balt likes to exert his authority over *everyone*. If you step out of line then you pay for it, male or female. Frankly I don't think it's all that different to living under the President.' Bodi sees Flip's dramatic side is still going strong. 'If it's any consolation I think they really care about you. I've never had as much attention as you get from them. What was it that you did to get them to react like this?'

'I went to see my mum's twin sister in Primrose Hill.'

Flip shrugs. 'So what?'

'Turns out she's Thomas Cleaver's wife,' Bodi adds.

Flip laughs. 'Seriously?! Oh my god Bodi, that's insane. You're a total bad ass!'

'I didn't know who she was. I just thought she was another member of Populus. But she told me where mum was being held.'

'Really? Amazing. Well, for you. Not so much for her. You know, 'inside'...' Flip gabbles on.

Bodi and Flip sit together awkwardly for a while.

'We should just go, you and me. Check it out. We don't need to tell the boys. No one would stop two girls, would they?' Bodi expects Flip to say no.

'Okay, maybe. Give me a few minutes to think about it,' she says and leaves the room.

Bodi can hear Reed and Evan downstairs arguing over the 'bip bip bip' of some ancient computer game. She quietly makes her way to Reed's room. She thinks that something there might guide her in the right direction. And she wants to see that photo of her mum again.

She finds Reed's room comforting, even if she is mad at him for backing Balt's terrible plan. She scans the walls for clues but there's nothing. Photos become pixelated blobs of grey ink. How can Reed sleep surrounded by all this? It would give her nightmares. She drags his chair over to the window and sits starring at the photograph. She recognizes more of the faces now: a young Balt dressed in army fatigues but with a more genuine smile on his face and there just in the corner, Rose! Rose at the demonstration? Now that is a development.

'Seriously, B, what is it with you and my room?' Bodi turns to see Reed at the door. He is smiling though.

'Well, I felt an overwhelming desire to induce my own migraine, so what better place to start?'

He walks over.

'I'm still mad at you, don't think I'm not!' she says, but her face says different.

'I know, I totally get it. The big bad Balthazar cramping your warrior style. But I'm starting to wonder what would I do without you? If something happened, if you were hurt, or taken away?' Bodi feels suffocated.

'What if something happens to *you*? Did you ever think of it like that?' she says.

'Good point,' he concedes.

'It's not like I feel I'm being kept out of the game in the playground, Reed. I brought this to Populus and now I feel they're taking it away from me. I can't just sit on the side lines like some dopey cheerleader.'

Reed starts playing with her hair. Pulling the curls down and letting them spring back. 'Reed! Can you not just pay attention?!' she reprimands.

'It's just nice to have you back. All feisty and raging against the machine. The delirious Goth Bodi was scary.' His irreverence amuses her. He is so much more at ease with her now that she finds it disarming. His initial brooding meant she had kept him at a safe distance. But now the gloves are off.

'Focus!' she teases.

'I am focusing.' He leans in and kisses her on the lips. She steps back. She had sensed that might be coming but it still shocks her.

'You're just trying to distract me so that I won't do anything...' she loses the word as he kisses her again.

'Anything stupid? Is it working?' he asks.

'Maybe...' Bodi gently touches the back of his neck where the stubble of his short back and sides is already growing out. She feels so self-conscious of her lack of experience and worries if she is doing it right. She reassures herself hat they are probably both new to this. 'Stop thinking' she thinks. 'Just enjoy it.' And she is.

'Well that's a development!' Flip is back. 'I knocked but you two were too busy gnawing each other's face off to notice. Nice.'

Reed and Bodi step away from each other, slightly mortified that they have been caught out, by Flip of all people.

'Back again? Can't believe you have so much time for us Flip,' Reed turns the focus to Flip. He knows the easiest way to distract her is to get her to talk about herself.

'I think we should get going,' Flip says to Bodi. 'You know, for our walk.' They head downstairs and Evan comes out to meet them all.

'Your 'walk'?' Reed says and laughs. 'Very subtle. You're off to Kenwood aren't you? What exactly is your plan, Flip? You gonna wave your magic lip gloss at the Sick Boys and they'll open the gates and let you in. Have you even thought through what you're going to do or are you rushing headlong into things again?' Reed's tone is more than a bit patronizing.

'We're going and that's it. I know Mum is there.' Bodi is adamant.

Flip harrumphs, 'Seriously Bodi, you are terrible at this. What did I say about keeping things to yourself?'

'This is ludicrous. B you have to think things through more. Can't you just go with the plan, for once?' Evan and Reed block the door.

'No.' She tries to shove past them, her mind made up. Balt will be back again with some lame plan that will involve being a waitress or something and it will be even longer till she sees her mum. She needs to get things moving again.

'But what is your plan?' Reed confronts her. 'Just tell me what you want to do and we'll see if it will work.'

'I don't know okay. I don't know but I have to do something. Let me out!' The boys stand firm, there is no way she is getting past.

'Forget it. If you're going to do something then we're coming too.' Reed is surprised by Evan's change of heart. 'Come on. We can't let them head off into some nightmare situation.'

'We're fine, we can take care of ourselves.' Flip stands next to Bodi, arms folded. Together they are invincible, a two girl attack squad.

Reed steps forward and uncrosses Bodi's arms, taking her hands in his. She won't look him in the eye. 'Please B. Let's go back upstairs think about what we can do. Together. The four of us, right?' Reed looks at Evan who agrees. Flip shrugs. Bodi doesn't budge.

'I know you think I don't understand, that I'm being overly protective,' Reed says. 'But I do understand. I'd be just the same if I had a chance to get my dad back. Even for one day. One hour.' The words catch in Reed's throat. Bodi feels terrible. She hasn't considered the fact that Reed has lost both of his parents. She is steadfast, looking pleadingly at him. He caves: 'How about we all go up to Kenwood then and have a look round? You said so yourself, Rose's information is good. Why would she do anything but help? Ruby's her sister.'

With Balt and Sam expected back anytime, the four of them grab their coats and hurry out of the house. Flip 's excitement at their imminent adventure manifest as hilarious tiny squeals. Flip is growing on Bodi, despite the barbed remarks that land her way every other sentence. She reckons there is more to her than her snippy exterior. Bodi is sure that Flip's mum is not an easy person to live with and she seems like the last person that would be part of Populus, but perhaps they are the only option she has to survive. She doesn't seem like a natural coper. To look at her you would imagine she was more likely go the way of Rose and marry some security bigwig. Who knows how she got involved in all this. She will have to quiz Flip later about how Penelope had ended up where she is.

A few clouds loom ominously on the horizon but it's dry for now. It will take them a while to get so far north but Reed has thought of a plan. He stops short next to an old van and dangles some keys.

'What now?' Bodi is impatient to get going.

'Result.' Evan grabs the keys from Reed. 'Particularly because *you* can't drive and *I* can!'

Reed reluctantly hands the keys over to Evan. And Flip joins Evan in the front of the van.

'It's Sam's but he thinks I don't know where the keys are,' Reed explains. 'He only uses it for emergencies. But I think this constitutes an emergency, don't you?'

Evan turns the engine over but it's flat. 'You're going to have to push it guys.' Evan sniggers, he isn't giving up his spot in the driving seat.

'For get about it!.' Flip is not happy with the way this joy ride is turning out.

'Well, you can always stay here sweetheart and do your nails,' Evan mocks.

'Fine.' Flip flounces out to join Reed and Bodi at the back of the van. 'This is fun.'

It seems Bodi's sarcasm is rubbing off on everyone.

They give the van a huge shove but nothing.

'Sorry. Hand brake.' Evan yells and lets the brake go. The van rolls back towards them and they catch it just in time. Flip is hardly putting her back into it but Reed gives it a huge push and they gather momentum.

'Right, Flip, go!' Reed yells and Flip runs squealing to the passenger door. A few seconds later when the engine has kicked in Reed opens the back door of the musty van for Bodi and they bundle in, slightly hysterical.

Evan is fiddling with the van's ancient radio, trying to find some music but Flip keeps going on about a secret dance station only she knows about. Bodi sits up and leans against Reed. She feels safer, steadier. A lot more than she would have with just Flip, so she is glad Reed changed his mind. She looks over to him and smiles. She feels happy. Then she feels guilty for feeling happy.

She whispers to him. 'What you said back there, about your dad. I'm really glad you said it.' She tries to look at him but is embarrassed. 'I've become so self-obsessed that I think I'm losing any understanding of what other people are going through.'

'You're caught up in yourself because your world has been turned upside down. And it's frustrating,' he says perceptively.

'Yeah but I've been getting so worked up and I end up with tunnel vision, you know? But I'm not like that normally. I want you to know that. I'm not an angry person. I'm normally quite thoughtful but I think that all this has changed me. I don't feel like myself at all.' She feels better for getting that off her chest.

'I get it. Plus you're living with people you didn't even know a week ago and we're asking you to trust us, and why should you? We don't even trust each other most of the time.'

She thinks she trusts Reed but she still doesn't know how she feels about him. What he is to her? It is all so overwhelming. Are her feelings for him real, or is she looking for a port in the storm? She is enjoying her time with him, despite what led her to him, but she really feels her lack of experience. She is standing on a precipice and being with him might be too big a leap to take.

'Trusting people is difficult for me. I've been brought up to keep myself to myself and to not expect anything from anyone. It's hard to change that overnight. Pretty much everyone at Populus has been good to me, but I'm still finding it hard to believe that they have no ulterior motives,' she says confidentially.

On the street, groups of people have gathered around a line of posters that have been plastered along a hoarding each declaring 'Reclaim London 31 October' or 'Take your city back 31 October.' Above the text is a Black P in the middle of a gold peace sign, the brand of Populus. Bodi looks at Reed but he looks just as clueless. Four black vans pull up and TrueSec minions jump out to rip the posters down.

'Did you know about this?' Bodi asks Reed.

'Bodi, as if?!'

'Okay, sorry. Evan? Do you know if Balt has something planned?' Evan shrugs. 'You think he tells me anything?'

Flip shakes her head. They are all in the dark.

'That's *this* weekend. What's Balt up to?' Bodi wonders aloud.

Twenty silent minutes later they reach the park that surrounds

Kenwood House. They park among some abandoned cars on a side street. This is a whole different story to Green Park. The grass is patchy; flowerbeds are overgrown with bramble bushes and trellises carry rogue wild roses that have survived years without care. The trees hold onto the last of their russet leaves. The rest crunch underfoot, a multicolour carpet. It holds a certain wild beauty. Here nature triumphs over the city that has neglected it.

Flip seems tetchy. She is either scared of what they are about to do or Evan isn't paying her enough attention. Bodi can't tell. Evan is wound up, marching backwards and forwards punching one hand into the other.

He turns to Reed. 'That's what he wants is it, more fighting? That march is like a death sentence. TrueSec won't think twice about shooting everyone down who turns up. It's not like the old days when you'd get sent hom with a slapped wrist.'

'Did you know anything about this Ev?' Reed asks. 'Have you heard this mentioned before now? I know they've all been meeting up a bit more than normal but I thought that was about Bodi's mum.'

'Nothing at all! He can't be serious. As if life's not hard enough now we have Populus plastered everywhere and they'll be trying doubly hard to get to us before that march happens.'

Bodi tries to rationalise it: 'What if it's like some rogue group.' She recalls Sam telling her about how badly that turned out last time, and shivers.

'You think my dad would miss a chance to get involved? He still won't accept the fact they lost last time.' Evan says, tetchily. 'But, you know, we're all old enough now, just right to help him reach a whole new generation of dissatisfied customers.' His cynicism is palpable. 'Hell, he's been training me all these years but I didn't think I'd actually have to lead the next revolution!' He shakes his head.

Bodi goes over to him. 'We don't have to. We don't have to march, or fight, or be the face of it. He can't make us.'

'Yeah right Boo. I can't see me being allowed to get away with it, can you? Where would I go? I'd be out on the streets.'

She touches his arm and he stops pacing. 'We'll have to talk to him later. We're here now. Let's at least take a look around and see if we can gather any intel.'

Evan smiles. 'Intel? Really?'

She laughs. 'Just for you Ev. It appears I'm a soldier in training, albeit without my knowledge, so I'd better get with the programme. Right, if we get seen, the cover is that we're just bored teenagers out with our boyfriends trying to find like a make out spot or something.' Flip's eyes light up. 'We just want to see where things come and go from, delivery bays, if there's an outside space, like an exercise yard, how many guards there are, that kind of thing.'

Reed steps in. 'Let's just get on with it. First sign of any real trouble just run, don't wait for anyone else. We haven't got IDs and we don't want to be held, that won't do anyone any good, least of all Bodi's mum. We'll go this way and you guys go that way. We'll meet up on the other side in half an hour.'

Reed and Bodi set off and climb up a small hill. The institution lies just above them so they have to be careful where they position themselves. A lone magpie overhead catches Bodi's attention, she quickly salutes him but he flies off. 'One for sorrow' rattles round her head. Not a good sign.

Lying down on the ground behind some trees they take in the scene. Bodi was anticipating a high tech, high security set up but the building is ramshackle. In a makeshift yard lit by dazzling floodlights one guard is marshalling a handful of prisoners, none of which appears to be Ruby. The prisoners wear grey tracksuits that have seen better days, dirty and saggy, held up with belts. The fence has barbed wire running along its top, the buildings have metal spikes around the edge of their roofs. They will not be able to get anywhere near. Reed takes out a tiny notebook and draws a sketch of the layout of the buildings, as much as he can make out. It looks more like a nursing home than a maximum-security prison. There are lots of small barred windows and security cameras covering the grounds and surrounding park. There are only a couple of guards but those that they can see are carrying guns.

'We should go,' she mouths to Reed, realising she's got them in over their heads. He shrugs, confused. 'It's too dangerous.' She makes the shape of a gun with her right hand.

'Two more minutes, I'm nearly there.' He taps his notepad with the end of his pencil.

Bodi lies still while Reed draws. She is worried about Flip and Evan and hopes that they have had the sense to make a break for it before now. She hears a rumble as a black van reverses up to the gates of the yard. Reed puts his head down and Bodi lies flat against him. They watch as the back of the van is opened and the driver and a guard go into the building. Moments later the guard leads out a group of prisoners shackled in hand and ankle cuffs. The jar of the metal restraints rings across the empty park. As far as Bodi can see there are two burly women followed by one very small one. The first two women hold their heads up but the third woman's is bent over. Her shoulders hang, the grey track-suit trousers drag on the floor, her red hair is cropped short in clumps on her head. Before Reed can stop her Bodi screams out: 'Mum! Oh my god, Mum!'

The woman turns her head towards the sound. Gaunt with black eyes, her lips dry and cracked, confused as if she has imagined what she is hearing. Reed tackles Bodi to the ground and puts his hand over her mouth. 'Shhh B.' The guards react instantly, orders fire out of radios, they head out towards them to investigate. The prisoners are bundled brusquely in the back of the van, the doors slammed shut and the guard and driver jump in and start the engine.

'Run!' Reed hisses at Bodi. A claxon's brutal wails scream across the park. All around them huge lights pop on one after the other, like a dramatic opening night. They can hear dogs barking and within seconds guards are rushing out of the gates their hands on their gun holsters. They have been naïve to think the building is poorly guarded. The guards spill out of the gates, spreading like a virus. Reed pulls his hat down to cover his face and pulls Bodi up to her feet. They run down the hill, tripping on rocks and grazing their hands as they grab at tree branches. They can feel the presence of the guards behind them, hunting them down. Bodi can't catch her breath and Reed drags her along by her hand. Down below them they can make out Flip running ahead of them, but where is Evan?

The black van holding Ruby speeds away down the road below them. Bodi's natural instinct is to follow it. She can't lose her again. How long will it take to find her? But Reed keeps dragging her away, down the hill and through the park. She feels like her lungs are on fire, her sides ache and her nails are digging into Reed's hand. They have to get down to the main road. They can disappear there. The gates to the park loom like a winning line but as soon as the van passes through it the gates start to close. They see Flip slip through once the van is clear and they use all their might to get there before the gates close. The fences around the park are high, something that they hadn't paid much attention to when they first arrived.

Reed gets through the gate just, and tries to hold the gates open for Bodi to squeeze through. The guards are seconds behind. Bodi isn't sure she is going to make it. 'You go!' she pleads with Reed. He braces himself to hold the gate open, his teeth clenched. The guards are there and ready to pull their guns on them, when a shrill wolf whistle rings in the air. Turning, Bodi sees Evan behind the guards shouting and brandishing a knife. All the guards train their guns on him now.

'Come on you Sick Boy dicks. Let's have you!' he shouts.

'No Evan! No! Run!' Bodi screams at him as she feels Reed pull her through the gate. She wants to stay and help but he drags her away. Tears stream down her face as her feet propel her further from her mum and her friend. She pulls back on Reed's hand but knows she has to keep running.

A single gunshot fires.

Reed's eyes pop out of his head, his grip tightens on Bodi's hand. Bodi strangles a scream. They get to the main street, stumbling like zombies bumping into startled passers-by, eventually turning into a side street and slumping in a doorway.

'Oh no, oh no, oh no!' Bodi sits rocking and muttering to herself. Reed is silent. She looks up at him. He too has tears running down his face.

'We have to go back,' she whimpers.

'We can't.' The words catch in his throat.

'We have to. Reed. Please?!' she begs.

'No B. No way.' He is trying his best to be the strong one. He stands up, wiping his eyes with his sleeve. 'Come on. We need to go.'

Bodi feels a rush of salt in her mouth, her pulse is beating so strongly it interrupts her vision like a camera shutter. She throws up on her feet.

Reed pulls Bodi up from the step and she staggers forward. He wraps his arms around her while she sobs into his shoulder.

'What have I done?' she cries.

Reed and Bodi see more posters for the march as they drive towards St James's. Reed is concentrating and is scratching through gears pretending he knows what he's doing. He is glad to have something to focus on, but it gives Bodi too much time for her mind to wander. It seems like days not hours since they saw people stopping in the street to look at the Populus posters. The news of TrueSec shooting a teenager has followed them like a tidal wave as they make their way south through the city. Bodi can feel the city prickle in her wake. She feels like everyone on the street is looking at the van. Like they know she is to blame for this terrible event.

St James's clock strikes eleven muffled chimes as Reed opens the door for Bodi; she knows the route now and leads the way. She crosses herself, this time in penitence rather than superstition, and they walk quickly and silently along the tunnel feeling both the relief of being safe and anxiety at what they now have to face. The thought of Balt's intense anger is almost enough to stop her going in, but she pushes the door open at the top of the ladder and goes to face the music.

Flip is already there, sat on a chair being interrogated. Her face is red and puffy. All eyes turn to them as the trap door slams down, and clouds of dust fly up. Like a mistimed magician's trick. Bodi can see Balt and the rest of Populus looking behind the two of them in the hope that the rumour isn't true and all four of the teenagers have made it back unscathed. Sam reaches down behind her to help Reed out of the tunnel. Bodi steps back away from the group, feeling the full force of the anger and disappointment in her. Sam reaches over to touch her arm but she shrugs him off. This is her fault; she is going to take the punishment.

'You did this! I hate you!' Flip screams at her.

Penelope has her arm around her daughter, she shakes her head with contempt. Balt points towards the vault and she follows him in there, alone. She can hear Reed's protestations being quieted by Sam. This is between Boudicca and Balt.

They sit opposite each other on folding chairs. Bodi braces herself for the shouting that is to come but Balt sits staring at her saying nothing. It is only when she takes a deep breath and tries to explain that he cuts her dead.

'This is what happens when silly children get involved in adult business. My son was shot because you couldn't wait a few hours. Because you couldn't follow a few simple instructions, little girl.' Balt's tone is calm but icy. 'Can you comprehend, even for one second, what it's like for me to know that my only child is out there and hurt, or worse, and I wasn't there to prevent it? To take that bullet for him.' The word 'bullet' cuts right through her. Bodi hangs her head. She struggles to find the right words.

'Have you heard, do you know, whether Evan's...' she can't bring herself to say it.

'Dead? Injured? No, not yet. I've got everyone I can on it but TrueSec has clamped down. I can't get anything from my people on the inside. And who can we send to ask? Everyone is wanted for one thing or another. I can't even find out if my own son is alive or dead.'

'I know 'Sorry' isn't enough. I know that Balt. But I am. I'm so sorry.' He meets her pleading with stony eyes. 'When you wouldn't listen to me about Mum I saw red. And Rose was right, Mum was at Kenwood. But they've taken her off again. I don't know where she's gone.' Bodi doesn't think she could cry any more than she has today but a few tears more trickle down her blackened cheeks.

'Well I'm sorry Bodi because now we can't help you to find Ruby. This whole event has put pay to anything we had planned. TrueSec is on high alert. People won't talk because they're scared of the consequences. It's impenetrable. I thought the march would be enough to distract them. Give us some manoeuvrability.' He rocks back on his chair, staring at the ceiling.

'So it was you. You *are* behind it. Why?' Bodi hates that Evan was right.

Balt slams the legs back down on the floor. 'That's nothing to do with you now Boudicca. Everything that's happening in the world isn't about you or Ruby. Do you understand? There are greater things at stake here. You've done enough damage.'

She stares at Balt trying to read his emotions. Nothing registers on his face. No pity or sadness for her situation. She is nothing to him now. Worse, she is the reason Evan isn't there with them. It also means she has nothing to lose.

'Why was Evan following me Balt? Last week, before I even knew you? He told me.'

Balt looks caught out. 'I was trying to keep you safe.'

Bodi is unconvinced. 'From what? We were fine. We didn't need your help.'

'So it seems. You're doing a great job of taking care of yourself. Never mind who gets hurt in the crossfire.' Balt stomps out of the vault.

Bodi sits completely still, worried that if she moves an inch she will set more catastrophic events in motion. The quiet talking in the other room becomes more heated but she can't work out what is being said. Sam comes in and takes her hand. He leads her quietly out of the vault and past the Populus members' scowling faces. He walks her back to his house. Bodi has never felt so unworthy of someone's affection She looks for Reed but he doesn't come. Bodi guesses he is being interrogated now and taking the sharp end of Balt's wrath. No one wants to hear her side of the story. To them she is a selfish girl that has cost them one of their own.

The birds' evensong jars Bodi's skull like an angry eulogy. "You killed him." Sam goes straight to the hiding spot for his whisky and pours himself a quadruple. He slumps in a chair and disappears into his own head. Feeling dismissed, Bodi goes up to her room and starts to pack up her things. She has to leave quickly and quietly. Having so few possessions helps. She takes down the Map of Inspiration. It seems so futile now. How can these dead poets and singers get her through this? She stuffs it in her bag. She doesn't want to be inspired, she wants to crawl in a hole and never come out. She goes into Reed's room and sits at his desk, running her fingers over the sketchpad, pens and pencils that lie scattered around. She notices a tiny sketch he's drawn of her tacked on the lamp. She takes it down and stares at it. In it her face holds the nervous optimism of a few days ago. She finds a clean sheet of paper on Reed's notepad and starts to write him and Sam goodbye letters. Her emotions flood the pages time and again, her pockets fill with abandoned versions she can't leave behind.

'What's that?' Reed startles her. Bodi folds the paper and puts it in her pocket.

'Nothing. Just needed to write something down. Not important.'

Reed holds up a bottle of antiseptic and some cotton wool. He comes over to her and starts to clean up her face and hands where she has grazed herself running through the park. Her jeans are ripped at the knee and she has cuts along her forearms. He gingerly presses the cool compress down on her cuts and the sting feels like insufficient punishment for the damage she has done.

A sadness hangs between them. They are both in shock, of course, but there is also the weight of culpability. Bodi for instigating the trip to Kenwood, and Reed because Evan was the one to save Bodi, not him. Reed pulls Bodi towards the bed to lie down, she faces the wall and he lies behind her, a barrier to any further hurt.

'Sam?' Bodi asks.

'Swimming off the coast of Glenmorangie,' Reed sighs.

'Were they hideous to you?'

'Pretty harsh. Penelope was practically hysterical. Balt was just an asshole, as usual. But then, who could blame him?'

'I'm sorry Reed. I never thought it would ever turn out like this.'

'I know.' They lie still for a while. Bodi can feel Reed's breath on the back of her neck but he doesn't stroke her hair or hold her hand. They lie side by side not touching.

'What I don't understand,' he says. 'Because remember, you wanted us to leave when you saw the guns. Why did you shout out?'

She thinks for a minute, trying to find a way to justify doing something so rash. 'It's like you said before, you'd do anything, just to get one more moment.'

He reaches out and holds her tight as she cries for another boy.

*R*uby's scarf rubbed the top of her nose to the point of distraction. The beanie keeping it in place was annoying her as well, it was too warm to be so wrapped up, but she had to keep a low profile. As they approached Westminster she was worried one of her Mother's work colleagues would spot her and grass her up. Cal walked next to her, beautifully bare-faced and beaming that incorrigible smile of his, his hand firmly holding hers. They were a definite 'thing' now, whatever that meant. It wasn't like any of her family had met him. Just the thought of Cal and her parents made Ruby feel queasy. Oil and water didn't even cover it, more an uncontained oil spill across the ocean.

Between them they carried a banner Ruby had made that morning at the squat. They were putting her artistic talent to good use these days. She had met Calder outside St Paul's where some protestors had set up tents and been living for a few weeks. On the steps of one of the largest and most famous cathedrals in the world it was like the circus had come to town providing a show for the open-mouthed tourists queuing to see inside. Villages such as these were popping up in capital cities across Europe and they were getting featured on the front pages of newspapers worldwide. They were on the cusp of something big.

When she had unrolled the banner, the sophistication of its design had garnered lots of positive attention. Cal had been visibly proud of her but more importantly she was proud of what she had achieved. She had properly felt a part of things. Now her banner was one of thousands being held aloft. A sea of people rippled with bobbing slogans. And Ruby and Cal were right in the middle of things.

They had got separated from the rest of their friends. And it was 'their' friends now, not just his. Being inquisitive and naturally open to ideas, Ruby had begun to fit in really well with the gang at the squat and she was spending more and more time there. Sam had taken on the mantle of her older brother and he kept an eye on her as well as Cal. She had made fast friends in a girl from Scotland called Morag who was a bit more of a hippy than Ruby could usually handle but she was very sweet and there weren't that many girls at the squat beyond the randoms that Sam dragged home from the pub. Pierre was a trustafarian that endlessly mocked her fancy accent though Ruby had her suspicions that he was more bourgeoisie than radical himself. And she was even growing to like Balt. He was a funny one. He hadn't quite worked her out yet so was keeping his distance, but she could tell she was growing on him. He had told her that morning that he was glad she was 'committing to the cause at a time of great necessity'. It was opaque phrases like these that really didn't help his standing in the squat. That and the fact he dressed like a total, A1 dork. Ruby would hazard a guess that he ironed his underwear. Or his mum did, anyway. But he was at every event, every meeting, any time she visited the squat he was there, trying to goad people into a discussion about the state of the nation. Even first thing in the morning, which was no mean feat before everyone was fully caffein-ated. He was nothing if not consistent is his relentlessness. And so Ruby was getting used to him, like an irritating itch that you learn to live with. Much like this scarf.

Ruby looked up at Cal. She still got hot and bothered when she realized he was hers. Well not hers, no one is your property, but she had shares in him and he in her. Even here, at the heart of the city surrounded by thousands of people, he carried himself like a chilled out surfer on the way to the beach to catch an awesome break. Cal seemed free and easy at all times. He knew what he wanted and more often than not he took it, rarely second guessing himself. His confidence was such a turn on. As cocky as Ruby could be she always had niggles that thwarted her. Her angels and demons raged a constant war across her shoulders.

Ruby was jolted from her thoughts by a rage of sirens. And the heavy thud of hundreds of heavy boots hitting tarmac. Cal's face instantly dropped its nonchalant air. He grabbed the banner pole from her hand and pushed her through the crowd. But he was too late. The police had formed a wall of riot shields around them on all sides, ket-tling them in. There was nowhere to go.

In a flash, previously passive protesters started shouting angrily. People jostled around her, elbowing each other in an attempt to es-cape. Like trapped wild horses they paced round and round the en-

closed area, pushing back against the police. Cal dropped the banner and wrapped his whole self around her. She felt his heart racing and his breath quicken. The crowd's shouting was thunderous. But rather than being scared Ruby felt completely exhilarated. She pushed free of Cal's protective embrace and stepped forward, pulling down the scarf from her face and screaming in the policemen's faces: 'Let me out! Let me out! Let me out!'

SATURDAY

She tiptoes out of Reed's room knowing that she has a small window of time to get her things and leave without disturbing him or Sam. She gets her backpack from under her bed and creeps down the stairs. Sam is asleep in the library chair snoring loudly, a half-drunk bottle of whiskey by his feet. She puts the letters on the kitchen table and leaves, closing the door to Populus behind her. She knows she has to leave them. She is no good for them, no good for anyone.

There has been a night of civil unrest in reaction to the shooting. The remains of fires burn on corners where hoardings have been ripped down and set alight. The smell of charred wood and burned plastic hangs in the air. Graffiti is scrawled across official buildings. Shops have been looted for the little they have and street lamps have been smashed. It smacks of a job not yet finished. The anger has yet to be satiated by these acts of destruction. The shooting has sent everyone into free fall.

Curtains are drawn, blinds down. Bodi has the empty streets to herself. Her boots crunch down on broken glass. It is barely a week since she walked through Green Park and Bodi, and her city, are unrecognisable from their earlier selves.

She keeps to side roads and out of sight of the police, processing the previous day's events. Her sadness overwhelms her but a new emotion is taking over. Anger. She knows it is her decision to leave. If she had stayed then she, Sam and Reed would have muddled through somehow as long as she learned to live without her mum. But Balt telling her they would no longer help to find Ruby is all the incentive she needs to leave Populus. She is not giving up on her mum yet especially now she knows she is alive. Someone has to fight for her and Bodi is the only one on the planet with the will to do it.

She heads to the one place she has left to go. The sun is nearly up when she reaches the house. She can hear movement in the kitchen and she knocks on the door of the service entrance. It is opened a crack and Jasmeet's face peers out. She slides the chain across and hurries Bodi through to the kitchen and then into her room. She sits her on the immaculate bed, everything in exactly the same place as the last time she had been there. Jasmeet locks the door behind her as she leaves.

The next thing Bodi knows, a shocked looking Rose is shaking her awake. Rose pushes the sleeves on up Bodi's top and looks at her bloodied forearms. Jasmeet stands by her holding a first aid kit.

'I'm fine, honestly.' Bodi sits up, pushing her sleeves down again.

'What are you doing here Boudicca? What happened to you?' Rose says.

'I got into a fight with some trees.' She rubs the sleep from her dark eyes.

'You know you can't be here.'

'I know and I'm sorry. But really, I have absolutely nowhere else to go in the whole world. This is it. This is my last resort.'

'Populus?'

'I don't know if you heard a little shooting yesterday, up at Hampstead? I was there. In fact, I think it was my fault.'

Rose looks aghast.

'I'm not 100% on that last point by the way. I've got my theories.' Bodi taps the side of her head.

Rose is obviously not in the mood for her dry humour and Bodi isn't quite sure why it is coming out like that. She intended to be polite and gracious and charm her way into her aunt's good graces.

'So you thought you'd come here? To the home of the head of the S.I.C.? I thought you were a bright girl.'

'Well, when you put it like that! Probably not the greatest plan known to man...' Bodi laughs. The absurdity of it all has caught up with her and she is feeling slightly manic. 'Is he here, your husband?' she asks.

'No, he's been at work all night and won't be home soon. There's been some major trouble on the streets. Well, it would seem you know all about that. Jasmeet, clean clothes please for my niece.' Jasmeet goes out of the room and returns with some white underwear and a grey cashmere tracksuit. It is the luxury version of what Ruby had been wearing the day before. 'Jasmeet will wash your things. Leave everything else here when you've changed and join me upstairs. Jasmeet will show you the way.' Jasmeet picks up Bodi's bag and takes it out of the room.

Bodi strips down and gets in the tiny shower. It has been so long since she has stood under a steady stream of hot water, it feels like a delicious indulgence. She lets the water flow over her for a few minutes and then begins scrubbing the grime away. She examines the grazes on her arms, a smarting reminder of yesterday. Rose's clothes feel extremely soft and smell clean and fresh. Bodi realises that she must smell really bad, a major assault to the senses in a house like this, whereas at Sam's she has just contributed to the general male funk.

Fresh faced and with her damp hair trailing down her back she goes into the kitchen where Jasmeet hands her a bowl of cereal and a glass of fresh orange juice. She devours it in seconds. She has been brought up with better manners than this but she hasn't eaten for hours. 'Scrummy,' she garbles, with a mouth full of food.

'Miss.' Jasmeet walks out of the room and Bodi follows her. At the top of the stairs they arrive at the hallway where Bodi first met Rose, a few days before. Jasmeet smiles and points towards a set of doors. 'Please.'

Bodi thanks her, 'Shukria Jasmeet.'

Bodi walks into the large drawing room. This is not a lounge or a sitting room, it is definitely a drawing room. Pale pink blinds barely keep the sun off huge chesterfield sofas drowning in cushions. A large, upholstered ottoman holds vintage copies of Vogue and Country Life laid out in neat lines and a small fire burns in a huge grate. The heady smell of hyacinths fills the space. Bodi feels immeasurably out of place. Rose gestures for her to sit at the end of her long sofa. A silver tray holds a coffee pot and Rose pours some for Bodi in a white china cup with a gold trim. It shakes in its saucer when Bodi takes it from her. She places it on her knee to steady it. She can't relax and sits upright and awkward on the edge of the sofa. For a room that is meant for lounging it is impossible to do anything but perch nervously like a debutante about to be presented to royalty. Bodi stares round the room taking in the paintings and photographs, the objets d'art and ephemera of another world.

'You have a very nice home,' Bodi says.

'Thank you Boudicca. That's kind of you to say,' Rose smiles.

'Is it okay for me to be here?'

'For now, yes. But do keep away from the windows, the guards are on red alert so are overly tetchy. And you will need to keep to downstairs. Thomas never goes below stairs and you already know Arthur so that shouldn't be a problem.'

'Arthur?'

'My driver. He carried you here when you were ill.'

'Oh right.' Bodi looks round again. 'You wouldn't think two sisters could live such different lives.'

'Not so different.'

'Really?' Bodi doesn't understand. Her aunt seems to have all the trappings of a happy life.

'Both trapped in circumstances beyond our control.'

'Though one looks like this!'

'Yes, one looks like this.' Rose said, resigned.

Bodi gets up and walks round the room. She picks up some silver-framed photographs. Most are posed, stiff portraits. Her uncle looks heavy set, bald with the requisite TrueSec moustache. They look far from a couple in love. More like actors playing the role of husband and wife.

'Got any kids? Any cousins I didn't know about?' Bodi asks, searching for photos of children.

'No we don't have any children.' Rose's voice catches. 'But such is life, it's not meant to be.' It sounds to Bodi like a well-worn line.

Bodi picks up a small frame, hidden at the back of a group of picture frames. It shows a woman in a neat twin set and trousers with huge brimmed hat and sunglasses on, a large drink in her hand, she is forcing a smile. At her feet two small red headed toddlers sit on a blanket. Bodi picks it up and stares at it, turning it to Rose. 'You and Mum?' Rose nods.

'And our mother.'

'She looks familiar.' Bodi squints at it. She can't place her. 'Maybe it's just the family resemblance. Was she nice?'

'Is. And no, not especially. We were mostly an inconvenience for her.'

'Guess I won't be running to her for help then?'

'No I wouldn't advise that.' Rose gets up and takes the photograph from Bodi. 'I haven't looked at this for years. Well properly anyway. Daddy took that photograph. He's not with us anymore unfortunately. He was a sweet man. We were inseparable when we were little, your mum and I.'

'And when you were older.'

Rose looks confused.

Bodi continues. 'The photograph, of mum climbing the Boudicca statue on Westminster Bridge, I saw you in it too.'

Rose laughs. 'Oh my, that! Well needless to say my rebellious phase didn't last long. One look at that photo and I was put back in my place by mother. But Ruby, well she wasn't going to be told what to do. She was never going to tow the party line. That day was nearly the last time that I saw her. It was like half of me was taken away when she left for good.'

'When was the last time you saw her?'

'We met just after you were born. I didn't even know that she was pregnant. She got word to me that she wanted to meet so we met in a café and there you were. She had you attached to her in an old Indian sling and I couldn't see you at first hidden away in all that fabric but when you woke up she gave you to me to hold and you were the most beautiful baby I had ever seen.' Rose smiles, wistful for that day. 'Mother got wind of me seeing her and that was it, the last time I saw my sister.'

'How did she find out?' Bodi asks.

'Oh, she has her ways, believe me. The less you know about that the better.' Rose puts the photograph back behind the other frames. 'So did you get to see Ruby?'

'She was there. I saw her very briefly, but they were moving her on to somewhere else. And I couldn't follow her because she was taken away in an S.I.C. van and well, then the shooting.' Bodi stops and takes a breath. 'So I don't know, is there anything else you can do? Can you go back to whoever gave you the information before?'

Rose shakes her head. 'Those bridges are burned I'm afraid.'

'It's so frustrating. Selfishly, I want mum back so badly. But from what I've learnt over this past week, there's a part of me that wonders does it make any difference if she is in prison? Is it right that she's there now for things that happened so long ago? I don't know. I've come to grasp the reality of what she was caught up in. We wouldn't have been in hiding all these years otherwise. Populus did some terrible things.'

'We were very young Boudicca, not much older than you are now. Ruby was so idealistic and she had a good heart. But she was also naïve and got too deep into something that was very… seductive. Everything moved at such great pace around Populus. By the time she understood the consequences of her actions it was too late, she had no choice but to stay with them. They were the only ones around to protect her. Even when I saw her with you as a baby she knew she had to get you away from them but she was worried how you were going to live. I couldn't help her at the time. I only wish I could have, but I didn't have any of my own money and my life went from being controlled by my mother to my husband.'

'But you managed to get out without consequences.'

'I was never really 'in' to begin with. I went along for the ride a few times, but I didn't have the passion for change that your mum had. I didn't like to rock the boat and Ruby was so busy rallying against our upbringing that I pretty much went entirely the other way to compensate.'

'And now this?' Bodi gestures round the room.

Rose shrugs. 'There are two sides to every coin.' She looks at her watch. 'I think we need to get you back downstairs. Thomas could be home at any minute.'

'But I can't just sit there hiding. I need to do something. Something about Mum or Evan. The boy who got shot.'

'Look what happens when you go off without thinking things through. And it's not safe out there on the streets. Things are really starting to get dangerous. It's like history repeating itself.'

'Balt started it again. I think he's determined to see it through this time.'

'The problem with leaders, of any kind, is that they rarely do anything for the good of anyone but themselves.' Rose said conclusively.

Rose ushers Bodi downstairs to Jasmeet's room. Next to her empty backpack Jasmeet has laid out the Map of Inspiration. Rose leans over it, smiling.

'Still worshipping her 'Gods of Inspiration' I see! She used to have tonnes of notebooks like this when we were teenagers that she had to hide from mother. When we went to bed she used to tell me the stories behind each of her heroes. I always wanted to be as passionate about something as she was but it just wasn't in me. She absorbed everything around her and searched for the light and the righteous in the world, and as a consequence she glowed. I was a dim candle to her beacon. Only so much light to go around I suppose.' Rose runs her fingers over some of the images, enjoying the nostalgia. 'I'd forgotten about this. I think I have one of her old books somewhere. I'll see if I can find it for you.'

A car door slams making Rose and Bodi jump and Rose leaves the room hurriedly. The lock clicks behind her. While the city rages around them Bodi is locked in a basement with nothing but time to think about what to do next.

Bodi takes a step back from the Map of Inspiration and stares hard trying to see a pattern or a bigger image. She always thought that it held secrets beyond the heroes and poems and drawings. That it could give her the answers she is looking for. She tries to mentally impose some different orders on there – the old London Underground map, her vague knowledge of astronomy, capital cities of the world, picking out the initials of all the famous faces to try to make words, picking out the names of places within the song lyrics or poems, looking for hidden objects in the paintings. She had done this a million times before when she was growing up. With only old records to listen to and a few books she knew backwards, she had to find some way to amuse herself during long evenings. Every so often her mum would add an image or poem by another idol and Bodi would see it as a new clue to open up this hidden world. Deep down she never really wanted to solve the mystery, if there had ever been one, because once the secret was revealed the map would return to what it was – a tattered, old poster covered in a collage of magazine clippings and the whims of a woman in hiding. Without the mystery solved, it always had another level to it.

There is no piano music this time. Raised voices carry through the ceiling above her, the thud of heavy footsteps. Bodi sits in silence, making notes, moving letters round, drawing shapes created by the placing of the images, trying to connect the dots. Poems she knows by heart she dissects to a point where they make no sense and become words swilling round her head like an overflowing bathtub. Images of Ruby and their life together blend with words on top of snippets of music on top of paintings on top of photographs. This jigsaw has so many layers and ill-fitting pieces it is impossible to make it work.

Bodi stops. What question is she trying to answer? Does she really think that there is something hidden in this that can bring her mum back to her? Is she looking for justification for the things Ruby has done when she was in Populus? Is she try-

122

ing to understand her own actions of the past week? Or is she clutching at straws at a time when she has nothing and no one? She grabs the Map and throws it across the room. There is no great moral tale waiting to be revealed, it is simply her mother's fancy, which should be taken for what it is: memories of another, simpler time.

Doors slam overhead and the car starts again. At least the coast is clear for a little longer. Jasmeet opens her door and Bodi sits with her in the kitchen. A tray with a small salad, a green juice and bowl of pills sits ready to go to Rose upstairs. Jasmeet ushers Bodi to sit down at the counter while she takes Rose what seems a very measly meal for someone with means. Bodi tucks in to the hearty vegetable soup and crusty bread and butter that is in front of her. While she is here she intends to build up her strength. It is only a matter of time before she is homeless again. She won't be able to stay here and the reality is she doesn't want to. She feels more confined here than when she was in hiding with her mum.

Jasmeet returns and smiles at her empty bowl and clean plate. She pats her on the back. Jasmeet holds up the saucepan of soup offering Bodi more but she shakes her head. She indicates that Rose is resting, acting swallowing some pills and putting her head to one side on her closed hands. While Jasmeet clears the kitchen, despite Bodi's protestations, she tiptoes up the stairs to explore. With Rose out for the count, her husband gone and Jasmeet busy with chores this is her opportunity to see if she can find out anything from Thomas's study. She reckons he is the kind of man to have a study at home despite having a whole floor to himself at work.

There are only a couple of doors left to try on the ground floor. One leads to a smaller room decorated with feminine florals and blousy prints. This must be Rose's retreat. It is somewhere Bodi wants to explore, she is keen to understand her aunt more and more as her barriers fall, but there isn't enough time to go down that particular rabbit hole today. She goes across the hall and finds what she is looking for. The stark cold masculinity of her uncle's office. A huge glass desk rests on polished chrome legs. A black leather chair sits next to that on top of a single huge grey rug trimmed at the edge with grey leather. Nothing hangs on the flat, white walls except a brutal oil painting of speared bull, red paint drips nearly the full length of the canvas. 'Cheery,' Bodi remarks. Metal blinds let in slithers of afternoon light which splay across the room. A bank of cupboards run across one entire wall but with no discernible way to open them.

Bodi sits at the desk and looks around being careful not to leave any finger prints on the pristine glass surface. She gently nudges things around with her fingers wrapped in the end of her sweat-shirt. He has the same cold, posed photograph of him and Rose that Bodi saw in the drawing room. A copy of the London Herald lay flat, ironed, on the desk. No one believes a word it says. It has been the president's propaganda rag for years so people don't even read it despite it being free and the only 'news' paper avail-able to them. The headline reads – Peace restored in city – and shows a line-up of guards in full riot gear, styled like a Roman le-gion. Bodi sticks her tongue out at it.

There is some kind of antiquated computer on the table. Bodi has no idea how to work one. She presses a button and the screen flashes on making her jump. Below the corporate logo for TrueSec she is asked for a password. Worrying that any activity on this might alert her uncle, or worse his golf cart thugs out-side, she backs away from the box.

Bodi runs her fingers along the wall of cupboards looking for a way to open them. She leans on one by mistake and it pops open. She leans on another, pop! After a few seconds of closing and re-popping the doors for fun Bodi starts to rifle through the con-tents of the drawers inside. Row upon row of hanging files stare back at her. This is as bad as the room at the TrueSec HQ, only this doesn't seem to have a coherent system. Letters and memos are jammed in every way possible.

'Not such a neat freak after all, uncle,' Bodi mutters.

It would take all day, maybe two to go through all this and

she doesn't really know what she is looking for. Obviously the whereabouts of her mum, but she has only just been moved so she doubts even Thomas has that information here. She could look for information on Populus, but what would she do with that? She has walked away from them now. They are better off without her help.

She hears movement above her, a bath is being run. Her aunt's day is topsy turvy. And while the city is rising up about her she is luxuriating in a bubble bath. How can two sisters be so different? Jasmeet will be up soon to clear Rose's tray and so she has little time to shut all the doors and get out. At the final one she comes to she stops. Peaking out of the top of one of the files is something familiar, it is a photograph of her leaning against the Boudicca statue on Westminster Bridge. Her eyes widen and she pulls the file out of the cupboard. She sits on the floor and spreads out its contents. Photographs of St James's and Frank's Gym, of her entering the TrueSec offices, transcripts of the conversation she had had with Reed in the café, with Sam on the bus, CCTV images from Kenwood House, of her arriving at this house... Bodi curls up her knees into her chest. This isn't happening. She goes back through the file, there is a gap of a few years, but there are some images of her mum from when Bodi was around ten and back earlier and earlier, surveillance that spanned a dozen years. Bodi guesses there are more files where this came from.

'I actually thought that I'd lost you both, but then some helpful chap gave up your location so we were able to, how might one put it, re-connect.' Thomas's voice breaks the silence like a smashed windowpane. Bodi begins scrabbling all the photographs together and then stops, realising there is little point. She isn't in hiding anymore, and as it turns out she never was. Before her is a file proving that her uncle had known about her and Ruby's location pretty much most of her life. She stands up to face him. She looks round her for something, anything that she can hurl at him and make a run for it, but it is futile. He is a burly man and he has henchmen just seconds away.

He gestures for her to sit on one of the padded leather chairs by the window. Bodi walks slowly across the room. He closes the door to his study behind him and comes to sit opposite her. The family portrait definitely captured his softer side because in real life he is a brute of a man. His shaved head is red and veiny, his cheeks pockmarked, his bushy moustache flecked with grey to match his TrueSec military garb. When he sits his huge arms and legs spread so he appears almost spherical, his short, thick neck barely visible behind his shirt collar laden with stars and honours. His belt carries a handgun, a sheathed knife and a baton.

'He's not taking any chances,' Bodi thinks.

He leans back and puts his hands behind his head. An alpha gorilla gesture that doesn't go unnoticed by Bodi. She sits forward in her chair, her hands grip the edges and she tries to front him out.

'I'd introduce myself but it seems we're already acquainted.' She smiles her most disingenuous smile. 'We didn't need to creep around and hide at all.'

Thomas strokes his moustache with his stubby fingers. 'No, you did need to do that. We couldn't have the face of Populus and her daughter out and about bold as brass. We just needed to keep an eye on you. Firstly, my mother-in-law wanted me to keep an eye on Ruby to ensure she didn't start anything up again and then you decided to take on the family business so we could hardly let that go unnoticed.'

'I'd hardly say I've taken on the family business. What choice did I have? I had nowhere else to go once you'd taken Mum away. Why did you do that if you didn't need to?'

'It was processed before I could stop it. And, well, let's just say I was intrigued by the identity of the snitch. Very interesting. Thought I'd wait and see how all this would pan out. And it's turned out to be a very useful move in the end. Now all the rats are scurrying out of their holes. It's only a matter of time before we have them all and we can put an end to this sorry little annoyance once and for all.'

Bodi stares back at him; she feels a mixture of anger and anxiety. Between Balt and her uncle she has had no control over her own destiny. As much as she has lived a limited life, she has always felt that she was in charge of what little life she had. Up until this point. How dare they? How dare they remove what little free will she had? And now all her new friends, Sam, Reed, Evan, are all in danger because she and Ruby have unknowingly led the Head Sick Boy to their door.

It dawns on her there is no way he is letting her sit there and not carting her off without something in return. 'What do you want from me?' she asks.

Thomas smiles. His shiny white veneers jar with his rugged features. 'Well I have to commend you. You've done stellar work for me already. I have Balthazar's son and those wretches still in hiding will show their faces at this march on Tuesday.'

'Evan's alive?!' Bodi lets out a deep breath, which she has been holding for days.

'Yes the boy is alive. The guards only fired a warning shot but it was enough to startle the little lamb into submission.' Bodi knows her uncle is full of it, there is no way Evan will have given in so easily. She has to get word to Balt somehow, so Populus knows she hadn't got Evan killed. 'I see you're pleased he is alive. Perhaps you've formed some *attachments* along the way? I wouldn't advise it my dear. They are rabid sewer rats and as much as your mother liked to play the people's revolutionary, you hail from much better stock than that.'

As if on cue, her aunt walks in, her face flushed from her bath. 'I heard talking Thomas and, oh...' she stands frozen, open mouthed at the doorway. She looks across to her husband, fearful of his reaction.

'I was just having a little catch up with young Boudicca here. Why don't you join us Rose?' His icy tone discloses his protracted grudge about her betrayal. He is visibly enjoying this, like a chess master finally getting all his pieces in prime position, ready to make his final move and wipe out everything in his way.

BOUDICCA JONES AND THE QUIET REVOLUTION

Rose moves across the room, starting to protest. 'I had to help her Thomas, she had nowhere...' He holds his hand up, she is not going to get out of it that easily. He bends his hand down slowly and she follows his gesture to be seated. And silent.

'So it would seem dear niece that I have something that you want...' he raises his eyebrows expecting her to answer.

'Mum?'

'Yes, well done. And you have something I want...'

'Balthazar?' she ventures.

'Very good. Quick learner this one. So I think we can come to some kind of arrangement, don't you?' His voice is so smug Bodi reconsiders not throwing something at him. 'I need you to save me a lot of time and bother and get me that King Rat, preferably tomorrow before this march turns into a proper headache for me, so I can scoop him up and put him in a cage. And then you get to go skipping off into the sunset hand in hand with your mummy. Now wouldn't that be nice?' He rubs his hands together, pleased with his own plan.

Bodi is raging that she has been played so easily. What a hideous choice to make? She stares at him with all the venom she can muster. 'You bastard.' He brushes her insults off like dust from a jacket. He is far too happy revelling in his master manoeuvres. 'No way. No way am I doing that,' she protests.

'Then it's ta-ta to Mummy for good.' He pulls a sad face, mocking her from across the room. 'To be frank she's not doing so well. I wouldn't give her that long anyway...'

Bodi is horrified, her anger propelling her across the room to lash out at Thomas but Rose gets between them, protecting her from Thomas's raised fist.

'Thomas, please, she's just a girl. She doesn't deserve this. It was Ruby that started this, Ruby who joined Populus. Boudicca's just trying to survive.'

'Sit down woman!' Thomas commands his wife. 'Haven't you done enough, bringing *this* to our door? Into our home. Both of you, sit down.' He looms over Bodi. 'You're acting as if you have a choice young Boudicca. You don't. I will round up all those

128

Populus vermin eventually so either it happens slowly and your mother rots in prison or we do it quickly and you get her back before something irreversible happens.'

'I can't. I can't do it.' Bodi's voice is barely a whisper. As much as she has contempt for Balt, her heart is heavy with her fondness for the other members of Populus that took her in when she had no one else. She feels bound by the debt she owes Evan. Did Evan save her life, just for her to go and hand over his father? How can she face any of them again if she betrays them? But leaving her mum to die in prison is unbearable. She looks Thomas right in the eye.

'I hate you!' she spits.

'Well that's just a cross I'll have to bear,' he chuckles.

'His exterior is not even half as brutal as his interior,' Bodi thinks.

'I suggest you return to your 'best friends' asap and get this moving. There's little time and I need that march ended. And then, well, we'll see about getting you reunited with mummy dearest. You,' he points to Rose. 'I'll deal with you later.' He banishes her from the room like a naughty child. She leaves, turning over her shoulder to mouth 'sorry' to Bodi, her face fearful of the rage she will face later. Bodi looks down at the floor.

'How can I trust you?' Bodi asks.

'Look. I don't need your mum. She's no good to me now. She's inactive. Plus it gets the mother-in-law off my case. And that woman is a bloody viper. She's not happy at all about the situation. You'll get your mum and maybe a nice little place you can scurry away to. A long way from here. A long way from Rose.'

'And I want Evan back too. He's also no use to you, as soon as you have his dad.' Bodi chances her luck, such as it is.

'Quite the negotiator,' he says, a little impressed.

'And I need a guarantee. How do I even know Mum's still alive?' Thomas walks over to the window and lifts the blind and points. There in the street at the end of the drive sits a black limo with blacked out windows. The driver returns Thomas's nod and the back window lowers. Ruby looks out, disoriented.

'Mum! Mummy!' Bodi wails, banging on the window. Her mum turns to her, tears streaming down her sallow face. Bodi runs for the door but Thomas grabs her round her waist. She kicks and screams but he isn't letting her go. She is like a chew toy in a terrier's mouth.

'I hate you. I hate you.' Bodi screeches in his ear.

'This is getting to be very tedious. Try using some of your other 'feeling' words.' He laughs at his own joke and puts her back down. Bodi watches the car pull away, her hands and face pressed flat on the window. Bodi slumps to the floor. 'Okay. I'll do it.' The words feel like splinters on her tongue.

'That's my girl.' And he walked out of the room whistling, leaving her sobbing.

All the way back to Sam's house Bodi frets over what she is going to tell them. She might go with a little girl lost approach and hope they fall for it. But how is she going to tell Balt about Evan without telling him the rest of the story? Any mention of Rose, let alone Thomas, will have her back out on the streets. First things first, she has to see Reed and assure him that she is fine. Perhaps it is something they can work out together? Her brain is fried after seeing her mum but there is no way she is going to let Thomas win.

The streets are shrouded in an ominous quiet. People scuttle home while others wait behind closed doors for it to turn dark. TrueSec's brutality has added fuel to the fire and there will be no escaping more unrest tonight. Black vans patrol the streets, their tannoy systems threatening harsh punishment for any wrongdoers and Bodi joins those scurrying along, keen to get indoors before getting caught in the crossfire. Balthazar's timing is spot on. The disheartened citizens are more than ready to challenge the authority of the President.

Sam is out; no doubt Balt has the elder Populus members working on the march at the bank. Or he is off somewhere drowning his sorrows. Bodi finds Reed sitting on his bedroom floor cutting out newspaper clippings for his wall.

'Is there even room?' She makes him jump. He stands up and

smiles at her.

'I think there's like a square behind the cabinet.'

She can tell he is fighting the urge to come over to her so she walks to him and puts her hand out. He squeezes it.

'That's quite a poor attempt at leaving B.' He looks at the clock. 'Like eleven hours tops.'

She laughs. 'Yeah, well once you realise you have absolutely no-where to go… And the rioting seems like a great party and all but I think it's a little too pyro for my tastes.'

'And you missed Sam,' he jokes.

'And Sam. Can't leave Sam.'

Reed pulls her to him and she rests her head on his shoulder.

'Where'd you get to little B?' he whispers in her ear. She feels safe and happy. The guilt and the happiness all mixed up again. She steps back from him, saying nothing.

'How about tea? Seriously, I know what people mean now when they say that tea is good in a crisis. Plus I think Sam's drunk all the booze!'

They walk downstairs. 'Why so dark?' Bodi asks.

'Sam wants us to keep a low profile and the electricity's been a bit on-off. Next door mustn't have paid their bill. We'll have to reconnect to someone else's supply. Gas is still on though.'

Reed fills the kettle and Bodi turns up a camping lamp. It is like they have stepped back in time to an Old Masters' still life. Overripe fruit and old wine bottles take on a nostalgic hue. The piles of washing up and dirty clothes disappear in the gloom. Bodi grabs a blanket from the library and wraps it round her shoulders.

'Did this house relocate to the Arctic while I was away? I swear it's getting worse…' She makes tense small talk with Reed while she deliberates in her head what to tell him about her day. She knows that he isn't entirely trusting of Balt but recent events mean that Populus have been brought closer together. He might not be that ready to work with her, who he has known all of a week, against Balt who he has known all his life. But she has to tell him about Evan.

They sit down next to each other; hands wrapped round mugs of hot steaming tea. 'I'd offer you a sandwich, but oh yeah, we don't have any food. Again.' Reed looks at her. 'So, the worst runaway in history, what's the story?'

'Right, erm…Evan isn't dead, in fact he's not even wounded. The shot they fired was a warning shot. They just have him in custody.' She avoids eye contact with him.

'Okaaaay. And you know this because…?' Reed has learned Bodi is full of surprises but this is next level.

'I went to see Rose.' Reed's eyes widen. 'And I may have inadvertently met my uncle…'

'Oh no Bodi. Are you insane? I mean amazing about Ev and everything, you know like a total bleeding miracle, but what the hell. Thomas Cleaver!' And then the penny drops. 'And yet you're back here? How does one get back here after meeting Thomas Cleaver?'

'Err, right, so don't go insane, but I may have made a pact with the devil.'

Reed ducks down. 'Are they outside? Am I getting taken away?'

'Nothing like that. You're quite safe.' She pats his hand and he sits up to his full height again, flushed with embarrassment.

'Then what? What have you done B?' his voice sounds so sad, disappointed. Like his whole world has come crashing down. Bodi isn't sure what to say. How can she tell him the whole truth? But how can she not?

So she tells him everything, from the very beginning, and he sits listening to the deal she has made with Thomas. When she tells him she has agreed to hand over Balt to TrueSec he looks at her as if she is the worst person alive. And then he looks at her broken hearted when she tells him about her mum being dangled as bait. She tells him about Balt and Thomas having her followed and how she feels like the pawn in two grown men's game of war. She tells him about how she is struggling with what is being asked of her, but what is she supposed to do? All the while he says nothing and when Bodi finally finishes they sit together in silence, him with his head in his hands.

'There must be a way to turn this round. If we put our minds to it we can come up with something,' he says, finally.

'Oh god, thank you. I thought you might chuck me out again.'

'Again? You left Bodi. No-one threw you out,' he says, wounded.

'Yes, I left. But I'm back now and I really need your help. So will you help me?'

'B, there's nothing I wouldn't do for you, you know that. But literally, this is the most impossible situation.'

The back door to the house shuts, disturbing their powwow, and Sam harrumphs in. He looks at Bodi as if she hadn't left at all. 'Young persons.' He salutes them, doffing an imaginary cap. 'Everything alright?'

'Fine,' they chorus, as only those plotting can.

'Good. Good. Been a hell of a day.' He heaves a plastic bag of tins on the table. 'Dinner is served.'

Reed picks them up and sets to work on heating some beans on the stove.

'You'll be wanting this back.' Sam sits down next to Bodi and gives her a scrunched up piece of paper. It is her farewell letter.

'Yeah. About that...' Bodi cringes in her seat.

'It's all good Queen B. Everyone has their off days. It's a tonic to see you. I was worried about where you'd got to. It's a relief to know you'll have a roof over your head tonight. Unless that is, you're planning any more moonlit flits?' He tries to laugh but his usual twinkle is dampened. Bodi sees sweat is pouring from his forehead. He rubs his eyes rigorously, as if doing so will reveal a whole new scene once he opens them again.

'You okay Sam? You don't look 100%,' she says.

'Just a bit worn down by Balthazar's plans for world domination. He's not what you'd call a benevolent leader. More stick than carrot. But then, he's not quite himself either. No word yet on Evan. And in this case no news is bad news I fear. A sorry state of affairs.'

Sam dabs his brow with a handkerchief. Reed and Bodi exchange looks across the room and Bodi shakes her head. There is no point telling him about Evan before they have come up with a solution to the Thomas problem. It will mean yet more interrogation from Sam about how she found out and she doesn't want to lie to him. They can't ignore the fact that he is involved, so how can he be subjective?

'What's Balt decided to do?' Reed asks his uncle.

'You'll know in good time young liege. Balt's calling a meeting tomorrow evening for everyone, to reveal his master plan. Where's that dinner? We need to get battle ready. I bet Mark Antony never had this problem.'

Bodi reaches across the table and takes Sam's hand. He squeezes her fingers tight. 'Don't you go disappearing on us again young Boudicca. I realise being surrounded by such magnificent specimens of manhood 24/7 can send young damsels fleeing to the hills, overcome with the vapours, but give it time and you'll get used to it.' She laughs along at his attempt to lighten the mood.

'It's a challenge but someone has to do it,' she responds.

As he continues to hold her hand she wonders if this is what it feels like to have a father. Sam feels more like an uncle but he would have been a good father she thinks. Maybe he had children, she has never asked. She wonders if she will get the chance. After beans on toast and more tea, Bodi and Reed go up to his room to work on the plan. In the semi darkness the walls seemed to throb in and out like a dull heartbeat. Bodi sees fleeting demons scurrying between the words and pictures; the manifestation of her guilt at keeping the truth from Sam.

'We need some kind of decoy, for the Sick Boys. Something that suggests they've won, just enough for us to get Ruby and Evan back,' Reed suggests, pacing the room, his shoulders hunched.

'Or I negotiate with Thomas. But who or what do I have to negotiate with?' Bodi sits on his chair jiggling her legs. 'We're going round in circles.'

'What if I do nothing? Then what happens?' she asks.

'Then you lose your mum, Balt turns the march into a riot, people get hurt. Beyond us, beyond Populus. Inaction is not an option.'

'And us, what happens to us if I get Mum back and TrueSec takes in Balt? Do we live here with my mum? Could you even bear to be near me?'

'You're assuming I don't get taken in as well. They'll find a way to charge me with something. Just going to Kenwood with you might be enough. Look how well Thomas has played you so far.'

'And Balt. I still believe that Balt has a hand in this as well.'

She stops still. Her eyes have adjusted to the gloominess now, she looks up at him.

'The one thing I do know is that I would like you in my life. If you'll have me.' Reed stops pacing and smiles awkwardly. He has been waiting a long time for her to catch him up.

'Sure.' At a time of grand gestures, he is a man of few words. He looks at her face, acknowledging the darkness under her eyes, the tension in her forehead. She carries the future of the city in her hands. It seems extraordinarily unfair.

'We will work this out B.' he says, reassuringly.

She stays with him and has a few hours of ragged sleep disturbed by violent dreams of raging fires. Throughout them she feels restrained by an invisible force: her actions futile, her screams unheard. She wakes insatiate and screws her eyes tight, trying her best to grab a few more minutes but nothing comes, her mind raging with a million scenarios, none of which resolve the situation. She feels Reed's body wrapped round hers. They are as entwined as bramble round a tree. Their lives will change irreparably that day and neither wants to let go of the other before they have to. Bodi reaches out for the photograph of the two of them as young children sitting between their parents. Her mother's eyes dance with promise, in stark contrast to the dark pools of pain that have replaced them. And now Bodi too is far from the optimistic child she sees in the snapshot, Reed too. Their childhoods have been all too short and she finds she is angry with her mother for creating this life she can't escape.

You had a childhood before you decided to change the world, she thinks. You had a time of friends and family and just hanging out. But us? Look at us and what you've created for us. Look what good your little war did us. We had childhoods of fear and solitude. We distrusted everyone and had no family. We didn't ask for this but we got it anyway, no matter what we do we're stuck with your legacy. How can you leave me alone to deal with this?

The anger rises inside her like molten lava. Her mother. Rose. Balt. Even Sam. They created the chaos, binding her up in it so completely and there is no way out. She puts the photograph face down by the bed, keeping her tears inside, not wanting to wake Reed from his much-needed rest. She nestles into him, perhaps this will be the last time they share this quiet togetherness and she wants to savour it. He instinctively holds her closer and she imagines for just one minute that they have normal lives and that soon he will have to sneak out of the house before her parents catch him there and that he will whisper 'see you at school' as he leaves in his bare feet. And their day will be full of flirtations across shared classes, holding hands during lunch, and enduring PE lessons, before returning home to cooked dinners, parents chastising them about homework and talking to each other about bills to pay, friends to see and sharing a rare glass of beer. Everyone together and glad to see each other and lost in the minutiae of everyday life. It is a life that Bodi can only dream of.

Carefully manoeuvring herself free of Reed, she sits cross-legged next to the bed looking at him. His mane of hair is already growing back along with a slight stubble on his chin. In sleep, his face is stress free and she catches a glimpse of the man he might become. It is if by pasting all the anger and hurt and destruction of Populus on his bedroom walls that he has found a calmness within himself. He has exorcised it and he is simply a contented boy with a great life ahead of him. Bodi realises she has to protect that future at all costs.

'**A**ll I'm saying Reuben is that you're getting a little too into it, you know?' Rose was pleading with Ruby to hit the breaks. 'Too into it? How is that even possible?' she retaliated. 'You know, chugging down the Kool-Aid. Feet first down the rabbit hole. Caution to the effing wind. You haven't been here in weeks other than to sleep.'

'You sound like her!' Ruby said caustically.

'I do not! Don't always throw that one in my face. I'm genuinely worried, sis. Me. I am worried. It's like you've joined a cult or something. And I miss you.'

'Well, come with me. I'm leaving now. Come with me and meet everyone. Hear what they have to say and then make up your mind. Experience it yourself before you trash it.'

'At the march?' Rose's eyes filled with dread.

'Yes, 'at the march'. It will be fine. There are absolutely loads of us going down. It's going to be the biggest yet.' Ruby purposefully excluded the part about the kettling and potential violence. Rose stood there silent for a second.

'Okay then. I will.'

Ruby was annoyed that her reverse psychology had backfired. She had hoped that the thought of the march would put Rose off. Now she would have to take care of her and the group would find out more about her family and that was never going to end well. Oil and water was how she liked it. But she had thrown down the gauntlet and Rose had picked it up. Now what?

'You might want to change,' Ruby said. 'Seriously, it would be good if you were to reassess 'pink' as a whole.'

'Don't be such a bitch,' Rose said but she was giggling, nervously excited about joining Ruby on the march.

'Twin sister Ruby. Something that perhaps you might have mentioned before now?' Cal was flabbergasted.

'She doesn't normally look like this. Usually there's a lot more pink,' Ruby joked, trying to distract Cal from the situation. Rose was standing chatting to Sam, making Ruby's jeans and sweatshirt look neater than Ruby thought possible.

'Doesn't normally look like this. It's not her outfit *Ruby. There is another actual* you *standing there. A whole other same, identical, replica person as* you.'

'Oh get over it! It's just my sister. You've got Sam.'

'Not the same! Sam is not the same.'

At that moment Balt strode up to them, greeting them with a swift 'Comrades'. Cal simply rolled his eyes and walked away.

'You might want to rethink 'comrades' Balt. Not particularly new millennial.' Ruby suggested, and followed Cal over to Sam and Rose.

'Your sister was just telling me all about you Ruby. Very interesting.' Sam loved a bit of intrigue and, to be fair, another girl to flirt with. Cal stood next to him staring from one of them to the other, confusion written large across his forehead. Sam patted him on the shoulder, 'He'll catch up soon enough ladies. Right we're off.' They started walking.

Rose pulled Ruby to one side. 'Sam's so funny. He was just telling me about the time he went to Marrakech…' Ruby recognised that glint in her sister's eye.

'Don't even think about it Rosebud. He's had more women in his bed than you've got cute cat photos.' Rose's face fell. 'And it would be so weird. What with Cal. You know…'

'I guess. Shame,' Rose grumbles.

'And we're here to take action, not get action.' Ruby said emphatically.

'Very clever dear,' said Cal from behind them. 'Now about this twin thing…?'

'NO!' Ruby and Rose both shouted at him. They had heard that particular request way too many times in their lives.

SUNDAY

The house is still as the sun comes up but traffic rumbles in the background as the city does its best to get on with its day. Sam's snoring sporadically breaks the silence and a few hallway lights come on, the electricity has been restored while they slept. The kitchen radio hisses below them. Bodi thinks of her mum. Where is she right now? Has Thomas thrown her in some dark cell or is she being held cold and hungry in a flat somewhere? Bodi knows there is no way they will find her until Thomas deigns to share that information with her. He is the puppet master and she has no way of cutting the strings.

Reed half wakes and nuzzles into her shoulder. With his eyes shut he mumbles 'Beautiful girl.' He kisses the back of her neck lightly and goes back to sleep. Bodi feels her heart break into a million little pieces. She is going to miss this. She begrudgingly manoeuvres out of his arms.

She goes through to Sam's room. Photographs of him with groups of men and women plaster his walls. They capture a happier time of parties, barbecues and holidays. By Sam's own admission he was always along for the ride and here is the proof. Wine bottles and beer cans fill the photos as well as smiles, kisses and funny faces. Small children, beautiful women and a coterie of male friends bay for his attention. In every image Sam's charisma shines out.

His clothes are slung on the back of a chair. Bodi goes through his pockets to look for an old leather-bound diary that she has seen him flick through. She finds it in his trousers and leaves the room quietly to look at it under the bare bulb in the hallway. It is a diary of some ten years previous. Notes and appointments crossed out and dates re-written in blue, black and red ink. A jumble of years and haphazard events that amount to one man's unruly life. At the back she finds what she is looking for. She memorises the address and puts the book back. It is time to go and talk to Balt.

Balt is surprised and not all that pleased to see her at his front door at barely eight o'clock on a Sunday morning. He looks behind her anticipating that she has been followed.

'I came in with the maintenance guy. And I walked through the back roads. Plus the Sick Boys are a little busy, what with all the chaos you're causing. I think we're okay.' Bodi's bluntness unnerves him. He unlocks the wrought iron gate in front of the main door. There are bars on the windows too.

'Come in. Quickly.' He steps to one side, again checking to see if there is anyone around.

Balt's flat stands at the far end of a semi-derelict block. It is a good cover. No-one really knows which flats are inhabited and which aren't. It smells of mildew and boot polish and is dark, the curtains pulled against the daylight. Balt parts them an inch so they can see each other. The light reveals maps and plans, books, ledgers, pens, notebooks, all arranged around a huge table and covering all four walls. Where you would normally expect to see sofas and side tables are rows of filing cabinets. This is one man's private War Room. She walks round the edge of the room trying to decipher Balt's master plan. She sees her old flat marked on the map as well as Sam's house and her aunt and uncle's place. In a time of restricted information, he is very informed.

'You've been busy,' she turns to Balt.

'Things can't stay as they are. It's time that woman knew she can't hold us down any more.'

'The President?'

'If you can call her that. What does she preside over? A country that's on its last legs.'

'Don't you think you helped in that? You could say that you

were even instrumental in bringing her to power.'

Balt glares at her.

She hears a cough from another room, which startles her.

'Evan's grandmother,' Balt offers. 'She's not doing so well.'

'I didn't know.'

'We all have private lives beyond Populus, Boudicca. Something of ourselves we keep out of view,' he sounds a little sad.

'I guess so.' Bodi came here with the intent of confronting Balt again, to get to the bottom of things once and for all so she can make an informed decision about whether to hand him over. Seeing him here, in a home that he shares with his sick mother and a room nearby that usually would hold a snoozing Evan, she sees more of the man than the menace.

'And this?' she looks round at the walls and the table. 'You keep this out of view as well? Away from the others in Populus?'

'I don't expect you to understand, but being a leader takes planning and thought. To instil and maintain confidence takes forethought and its essential to turn up to things prepared.'

'No down time then?'

'When you believe in what you do then you don't need it. Populus is my life.'

'And what do you believe in Balthazar? What drives you to live like this 24/7?' Bodi is genuinely curious. So far their discussions have been on a more formal level. This is her one chance to see what makes him tick away from the bravado of fronting the campaign.

'Change is everything. Without change we are just stagnant, unthinking. We're irrelevant. We become the victims of our own procrastination.'

'Yet right now we're both thinking that a little bit of staying in one place might be a good thing.' Bodi forces a smile but Balt doesn't reciprocate.

He walks through to the kitchen and she follows him. No curtains hang here and she looks out the window across the city. They are high up, she knows that because her legs still ache from climbing sixteen flights of stairs, but the view is something else. The residue of the night's activities are still visible – small wisps of smoke rise from the rioters' fires, mingling to create a smog across the horizon, the sun streaming through it reminds the city's inhabitants that no matter what they try to throw at it they cannot stop the world from turning. She recognises the dome of St Paul's in the distance. It was boarded up years ago by a clergy that has long since fled to the countryside. The skyline remains unchanged from a distance, though close up you would see chain fences and hoardings, burnt out shells and graffitied monuments. Bodi wonders what force might be powerful enough to flatten her beloved city once and for all.

Balt heats some water on a small stove and makes them some tea while she looks out the window. 'It's so beautiful from up here. You'd never know the struggles that go on in every street down there. It's like stepping back in time to when things were good and happy,' she says.

'Depends what your idea of happiness is. When I was younger it was commonly felt that money and possessions were a mark of true happiness. But people didn't talk to each other. They didn't know their neighbours. They left the care of their own city to poorly paid workers. They lost their pride in the streets around them as they filled their homes with more televisions, more food, more wine. They showed the world who they were through what car they drove, the labels on their clothes, where they went on holiday, the size of their bank accounts. Charity began and ended at home. To their mind things were perfect that way, it made them 'happy' but spiritually they were bereft. No amount of holistic medicine and yoga could revert the balance. They were empty.'

'And that's why you fight?'

'That's why I want to change things. It wouldn't have to be a fight if we felt heard but everyone's ears are closed. Each man is for himself, even more so than before, because each man is trying to survive and to protect his family.'

'And you're just protecting your family?' Bodi feels there is much more to it than that. From what she knows of Balt his ego is bigger than the dome of St Paul's.

'Families, across the city, across the country. Giving them a voice again. So they can talk to each other and talk to government and live somewhere their voices are heard.' Bodi is a one girl audience to one of Balt's great speeches.

'And in the process you'll bomb some families and burn their houses and people won't be heard, because they'll be dead!'

'There have to be some sacrifices. And *you* know that, as well as I do. People get hurt when you upset the system. Go chasing after what you want.' Tears come to Balt's eyes. His passion for a new utopia is nothing compared to his love for his son.

'He's not dead.'

'What?'

'Evan. He's not dead. Don't ask me how I know but I do. It was a warning shot that we heard, that's all.'

Balt clasps the edge of the sideboard, relief flooding through him. 'Oh my.'

Remembering himself he lets go of the side. A steeliness reappears in his eyes. Father of the year is gone, Balt the great and all powerful is back.

'How did you get this information Boudicca? I can't imagine it was easily won.'

'I can't do that Balt. I wasn't going to tell you at all but you looked so sad. Well obviously. And I'd hate for mum to think I was dead when I wasn't. So that's it, that's all you're getting.' She tries to shrug off the situation, play it light-hearted in a 'hey, just be happy your son's not dead' way but of course he wants more.

'Look here little girl, you don't know what you're dealing with. You just don't have the capacity to pull off whatever you have planned.'

'Oh don't you worry, I'm a quick learner and I've pretty much got the measure of everyone I've met so far. It's like you said, every *man* is for himself.'

'A lot of people could get hurt if you carry on working on your own. Going off and disturbing things that should be left for experienced operatives to manage. You can only be doing more harm than good.'

'More harm than you're doing? Handing people over to the authorities, causing riots, persuading innocent people that they are an army?!' Bodi couldn't believe him.

'And there was I thinking that you'd be as useful as your mother and all you've done is stir up trouble and make things worse.'

'Useful?! Useful? I am a person you know, not just one of your silly toy soldiers. Exactly how long have you thought I might be useful to you? A week? A month? Longer? Are you even aware what impact your decisions have on people's lives, on their families? Collateral damage has a face you know.'

'I think it's time you left Boudicca. I have nothing further to say on the matter.' He cuts her dead. He isn't going to answer to her today. 'The mission is much more important than you thinking your privacy has been invaded. And now I have to work out how to get my son back home before anything happens to him.'

He marches her to the door and without another word opens and closes it behind her. Bodi is bemused by the two sides to the man she had seen: a concerned father and a brutal egomaniac. She trudges down the stairs. There is nothing else for it. To get her mum and Evan back, to stop the march turning into a huge riot, she has to give up Balt.

She takes a circuitous route back to Sam's. He is just up and bumbling about the kitchen. She brings in a pint of milk.

'Bodi, you should be careful. The skies have eyes you know!' Sam's sense of drama is still intact. 'But cheers.' And he takes the pint from her and pours half of it into his coffee. 'Now let's hear where you've been this morning. I don't buy this 'popped out for a pint of milk' crap for a second.'

So she sits and tells him what has happened and where things stand now. He soaks it all in as he sips his coffee. His face registers no shock, he doesn't judge her just listens, occasionally nodding, encouraging her to tell him everything. Bodi feels a huge sense of relief at sharing her troubles with Sam. She trusts him hugely and she also wants to give him a heads up as to how the day might pan out. And as it turns out, he has a few ideas that might avert total disaster.

Half an hour later Reed comes in, still bleary from sleep. He kisses her cheek while Sam's back is turned.

'I'm not as green as I'm cabbage shaped, young persons. I know what's going on under my own roof. Just keep it PG please.'

Bodi and Reed have no idea what that means but they get the implication.

'Sure boss.' Reed defers to his uncle with a laugh. Bodi smiles at Sam. He is pretty chipper considering the day that lies ahead. Sam leaves them alone in the kitchen.

'Where have you been? Really.' Reed asks.

'Nowhere in particular,' she lies. 'Wanted to see the city before it's burned to the ground. Again.'

'Bodi, we're in this together. We decided.' He sounds exasperated.

'It's best I do it alone,' she says. 'That way you won't need to act the big hero and get caught up in all of it. Also, you can say you didn't know anything to the rest of the Populus crew and it will be true. I want you kept out of it. I've decided. It's *my* battle with Balt and with Thomas. I appreciate you want to help but it's not fair to drag you into it. And I'm a big girl, I can take care of myself.'

'You're infuriating and stubborn, that's what you are. When will you get it into your head that I'm already caught up in this? You can't save me.'

'I can try.'

'So you have a plan. A fully formed and feasible plan? That you've thought through from beginning to end? Cos last night, well you didn't know which way was up.'

'Of course I do.' She isn't even convincing herself. And Reed definitely isn't fooled.

'I had better say goodbye then, because by the sounds of things it's all going to go tits up and you're going to disappear in a puff of smoke, much like how you arrived. Good luck with that.' He storms out.

'Reed…' she protests, but he is gone.

She needs energy for the day ahead; no time to think about boys' bruised egos. She grabs some cereal and eats at top speed. She has a plan to put into action.

An hour later she is back at Rose's. She never thought she would be there again but she has no choice but to deal with him face to face. TrueSec is on high alert so she has to be careful she isn't picked up for a minor offence along the way. Jasmeet is there, as always, and she lets her into the kitchen. This time she brings Thomas down to meet Bodi. Seems like Jasmeet knows everything that is going on.

'Ah, our little spy. How is the world of espionage today, dear niece?' Bodi shivers at the sound of Thomas's voice. She hasn't forgotten their last meeting. She hands him a piece of paper.

'3pm today, Blackfriars. Give me my mum and Evan, and I will hand over Balthazar.'

'No formalities? No 'Good morning dear uncle'?' he teases.

'You've got what you wanted. I don't think there's much need for pleasantries now, *dear* uncle.'

'Listen missy, don't forget I'm the one in charge. You do not dictate the time and place and you sure as hell don't get your precious boyfriend and mummy back before I have that wannabe Che Guevara in my grasp.' Thomas grows red in the face, veins popping at his temples. 'This is how it will go down. You will arrange for Balthazar to meet you at Blackfriars at *four* o'clock. Leave the rest to me. Don't worry, you'll get your mother back and the boy, well, he's not much use to me once I have his father. In fact, I have you to thank for delivering me another bargaining chip, that was very thoughtful of you. Now, shoo.'

He stomps out of the room banging the door behind him. Jasmeet opens the back door for her squeezing her arm as she leaves. 'Mr Thomas is a total prick!'

The city trundles on about its business. People step round the smouldering fires, the broken glass and bricks, eyes down but vigilant, taking new routes that avoid the groups of Sick Boys who are stopping anyone who looks vaguely suspicious. Batons no longer stored in their belts but held in one hand beating a constant rhythm in the other palm, ready to go to work. Their aggressive timpani grows in pace. The message is clear; a wall of violence will meet any one who dares to march. No questions asked. Bodi can see the delight in their eyes, knowing that finally they will get to exercise some power over those weaker than themselves.

She stops off at St James's on her way back to Sam's. She sits on the cold stone floor to compose a note for Balt. Morag and Fergus are surprised to see her head pop out of the trap door but say they will pass on her letter to Balt who is due any second. She refuses their offer to wait and runs off back through the tunnel before he can confront her on the letter's contents. The wheels are in motion and she has to keep once step ahead of things or else the plan will go very wrong.

Back at Sam's, Bodi feels conflicted about how happy she is at the thought of getting her mum back. She is breaking up another family – Balt and Evan, and beyond them the Populus family – to reinstate her own. She realises that she has become as selfish as them. She has had to think like them to beat them, but it doesn't mean she likes it. She justifies it by thinking she has no other choice, but does she?

Reed lingers in the doorway of her room staring at her, just like the first day they met. As if reading her mind, he says: 'You're becoming just like them. Your single-mindedness has blinkered you into thinking that all your actions are justified and they're not. I don't know the ins and outs of your plan but I'm sure that someone you care about will end up getting hurt along the way.' She turns away from him. How did he get so intuitive? He continues: 'These things are rarely straightforward. You only have to look at my bedroom walls to know the potential for human misery that rash decisions bring. Just think about what you're doing. If I can help you maybe we can think of a way to do this where no-one gets hurt.'

'It doesn't exist. Balt and Thomas have backed me into a corner and I can only make this right by fighting fire with fire. I'm sorry

Reed. I know that you want to help me but I'm beyond help. It's best you just forget I was here. Just remember me as that sweet little kid you knew during a long hot summer. And keep Sam close and keep each other safe.'

She grabs her backpack and squeezes past him to get out the door. Their eyes meet and she feels his sense of betrayal. She keeps moving, despite the tears pricking her eyes. She has an hour to get to the meet and it is right across town.

Bodi walks tentatively along the riverbank. The tide is rising and soon she will run out of beach. People come down here in the day mudlarking, to see if the river has left behind rare treasures that might change their lives, but she has little to give to them these days but plastic bags and cardboard boxes. Bodi had climbed down a ladder from the Embankment in order to get a safer view of the meeting place. Her naivety doesn't go as far as trusting her uncle.

She climbs up another ladder further along. No one gives her a second glance. She scrapes mud from her boots on the side of a rung and keeping close to the wall walks to the corner to study the entrance of the building. It is an old factory that has been changed to executive homes and back again. She stuffs her backpack in a disused telecoms box and wedges the door shut with a brick. A biting wind comes in off the river and whips right through her, mingling with her fear to freeze her to the core.

There is no one lingering but Bodi knows she is being watched. It is now or never so she jogs round to the front door and sneaks in. The lift door is open but furniture and boxes have been stuffed inside to make it unusable. The only option is to climb the stairs.

'Seriously, don't you think you're taking this spy thing a little too far.' Her uncle's voice booms down the stairs. 'Get up here now or you'll mess it up'

Bodi races up the stairs two at a time and follows her uncle into a small room. Two Sick Boys gave her the once over. The three of them are crowded round a monitor. Bodi pushes between them and looks at the screen, her jaw drops.

'You didn't say anything about Evan actually being here, I thought you'd just let him go from your cells.'

'I thought it might add a little drama to the proceedings.' And Thomas relishes drama.

'But he's been brought up to fight. I can't see him leaving here without him getting hurt,' Bodi protests.

'Well, then who could blame me for taking out a troublesome teen that attacks my men?'

'You promised!' Bodi knew she couldn't fully trust Thomas, but he is like a man eager to bet on a dogfight. The three men laugh at her.

'Well, let's hope he behaves himself.' He is enjoying this far too much.

Evan sits on the floor in the dark, tied to an iron column. His clothes are dirty and dishevelled, his eyes dark and terrified. He looks like he is waiting for an execution squad. With his knees to his chest he makes himself as small as possible, trying to escape the eyes he knows are watching him. Bodi feels her heart lurch. His spirit has been broken; she can see that even on this tiny screen. What have they done to him? She looks at her uncle and he just shrugs. He found a way to justify his behaviour long ago.

Bodi hears a noise. Someone is headed up the stairs as quietly as possible but the old oak stairs creak their welcome. Bodi's eyes are glued to the screen. Balt races over to Evan.

'Dad! Is that you?' Evan whispers in disbelief.

'Just a second and I'll get you out of here.'

Bodi realises she is alone. Thomas and the Sick Boys are on their way in, she runs to catch up. When she gets to the room Evan is standing up next to his father, fronting out the guards.

'Balthazar.' Thomas sneers.

'Tommy.' The men feign civility and Bodi sees the recognition in their eyes. This is not a first time meeting. 'I see you've made this a family day out.'

Bodi steps out of the shadows. Evan's shock registers on his face. 'Boo?'

'I'm so sorry Ev, I-'

'Shut up!' Thomas cuts her off and gets up in Balt's face. 'Seems your little plan backfired Balt. Getting Ruby out of the picture didn't quite go to plan.'

'I knew it!' Bodi is furious. 'You did it, didn't you? You told the Sick Boys where to find mum and me. That's why you didn't go ballistic when they took Evan! You knew deep down that it wasn't my fault, it was yours.' That is it. She has been sympathetic up till now but she's had enough. TrueSec are welcome to him.

'I needed a new face for the uprising. And who better to capture the spirit of a new Populus than Ruby's daughter.' Balt is very matter of fact about his actions. But Evan is angry, 'Bodi, you didn't think this through. They'll kill him.'

'Err, not right away.' The Sick Boys laugh at Thomas, he is really milking his part. 'Right enough of this. You' he points at Evan, 'time for you to make a sharp exit.'

'What?! No way. I'm not leaving him. Dad? I'm not leaving you.' Tears run down Evan's face. Balt lays his hand on Evan's forearm and shakes his head. Bodi knows that Evan will take whatever small amount of life he has left to fight these men who are taking his father away.

'Evan. It's time to go. I want you to go.' Balt's voice breaks a little though he tries to sound firm. 'You are also the new face of the fight.'

'Oh don't make me laugh,' Thomas sneers. 'What fight?! Without you, well frankly even with you, Populus is just a bunch of cranks with baseball bats and firelighters.'

'Seems we've got you scared though Tommy. Not quite going to plan for you either, is it?' Balt counters with a smirk. Thomas bristles.

'Junior, off you go, no time for fond farewells. I've got a march to stop.' Thomas has had enough.

Evan grabs his father and holds him close. He turns and walks past the guards, fronting them out but not fighting. The disgusted look he gives Bodi makes her stomach lurch. She hears him run down the stairs. The guards seize Balt and kick him in the back of the legs knocking him down to his knees. They put a gag in his mouth to muffle his groans. His eyes stare at Bodi, drilling into her conscience, before a sack is put over his head and his hands are cuffed behind his back. Bodi is visibly shaken by the brutality.

'What did you expect, kid? We aren't in the business of caring and sharing.' Her uncle gloats. She has done it now, there is no way to undo it.

'And mum?' Bodi remembers the business in hand.

'Sorry, was there something else I can do for you?'

Bodi stamps the floor in frustration. Thomas laughs. 'Oh alright then. Think you're going to have quite the surprise when you go to collect your dear mother. Quite the surprise. Right let's go.'

He hands her a piece of paper with an address on it. The guards march Balt out the room and out the building. Bodi waits a second and then runs out herself. She doesn't trust Thomas so she knows she has very little time. She reads the address again, confused.

She goes to get her bag from the telecoms box but it is gone. Turning around she feels it swing into her stomach, knocking her to the ground.

'Looking for this?' Evan is seething.

'Ev, you have to go, it's not safe.' She coughs and splutters.

'Yeah, especially when there are traitors everywhere you turn. Boo, what were you thinking? I just can't believe that you'd set my dad up, after everything. I almost took a bullet for you girl.'

'Really Ev, I'm so sorry. But there's so much more to this. I can't tell you now. I have to get going. But it's not the end. I promise.'

She goes to run but he blocks her way. She reaches out and puts her hand on his chest, holding him off. He is pushing against her but his heart isn't really in it.

'I understand what you're going through, honestly I do,' she says.

'Out of everyone. You feel like your guts are where your heart should be and your head is running at a thousand miles an hour. But they knew they could always get to Balt if they held you and you would've stayed locked up forever if I hadn't done something. I couldn't leave you there.'

'So you get your family back and I lose mine?' Evan's face crumples.

'Maybe. But it's not over yet.' Bodi kisses his cheek and starts running. 'Morag and Sam are expecting you. Go. Now.'

Bodi runs across town to Green Park. This is the last place she had expected to find her mum but that's what the address says. Clarence House. A grand address that had been home to royalty when London was merely a courtiers' playground. Bodi expects to be stopped at the gates but every guard, every member of staff that she encounters, lets her pass without question. In fact, they seem to give her a nod of acknowledgement. She feels part of some elaborate hoax. A housekeeper shows her up a grand staircase. The light from a huge crystal chandelier dances on the paintings and photographs that line the stairwell. Heavy silk curtains ripple in swags at the windows, hiding the bars beyond them. Bodi has never seen anything like it in her life. The housekeeper pushes open a door and retreats, leaving Bodi to walk through. A large upholstered bed holds a very small sleeping woman. The half-light of a small bedside lamp breaks the grey of dusk to reveal Ruby. Bodi rushes forward and throws herself at her mother.

'Mum, oh mum! You're okay.' Ruby doesn't move. With her cropped hair she isn't quite the same. She smells different too. A lingering chemical smell that challenges Bodi's memory of her. 'Mum?'

Bodi picks up a bottle of pills next to the bed. She notices a cannula inserted into her mothers arm connected to a drip.

'The doctor advised we sedate her, just while we get her well. Thomas really went too far this time. There was no need for her to be so badly treated.' Bodi looks up and sees a figure in the doorway.

'Rose?'

'No, not your Aunt Rose this time, though it seems you and she have developed *quite* the friendship.'

The woman with her aunt's build and a similarly strained voice moves forward into the light. Her grey hair is pinned up tight to reveal a face dwarfed by huge sunglasses, her face is pinched and she wears a plain, navy trouser suit buttoned up to the neck. A badge of office sits on her chest. Bodi stands up instinctively.

'Madame President?'

Now she is scared, what on earth is her mother doing here in the President's care?

'Boudicca. Let me look at you.' Her hand reaches out and lifts Bodi's chin, like a pedigree dog being inspected for flaws. The President's dark red nails graze her skin as she turns Bodi's head one way and the other.

'You have your father's nose. Not much we can do about that I suppose. Otherwise it's like going back in time.'

Bodi takes a step back. This is all getting way too weird.

'I'm sorry?' She looks at her mum, out of it, her head peeping out from heavy linen sheets and cashmere blankets, and then back to the President. The pieces aren't falling into place. Though something horrible starts to dawn on her. 'You are my...?'

'Yes, I'm your grandmother Boudicca. Edwina Chancellor. Boudicca. Your mother really was giving you a poisoned chalice with that name!'

'Grandmother. Okay...' Bodi is blindsided by this news. This is the woman she has been taught to detest more than anyone on the planet and now she and her mother are in her house. And they are related. She is her mum's mum. She leans on the edge of the bed reaching for something solid.

'Right er Edwina,' she says. The President scowls. 'Sorry. Grandmother. I have to go.'

'Don't be absurd. I have everything ready for you. Marie has drawn you a bath and I have some clean clothes for you. I think the people's revolutionary look went out quite a few years ago.' She tries and fails to make a joke. Bodi raises the corners of her mouth out of politeness.

'I should take Mum too. We need to get out, I mean, you must excuse us. From under your feet...'

'Ruby isn't going anywhere. Any fool can see that. I must insist that you stay also.'

'I can't do that. Just a few loose ends to tie up. But then, then I'll be back. Of course. For Mum. When she wakes up. And we can catch up. Because, well, BIG surprise all this. Insane, really. Relatives all over London it seems. Rich ones. Powerful ones. All a bit crazy.'

All the while Bodi is rambling she is backing round to the door. She gives her mother one last look and runs down the stairs. She has to get to the gate before her grandmother can stop her. She runs faster than she had ever run in her life but the guards are ready for her. She comes to a sharp halt when the ends of their guns are pointed at her. Looking through the wrought iron gates she catches a glimpse of someone familiar through the traffic, on the other side of the road. Watching. Expressionless. Reed.

Her grandmother stands on the front steps, her arms folded. It has been a long time since she had encountered disobedience. Bodi turns and drags herself into the house.

'It seems the apple doesn't fall far from the tree.' Edwina shakes her head in dismay. 'Let's try this again, shall we? Marie has drawn you a bath and there are clean clothes laid out for you.'

Bodi reluctantly goes back upstairs where she undresses and gets into the bath. The bubbles irritate her, the pleasantness of the room irritates her, the subtle light of the flickering candles irritates her. She tries to lie still but she screams out, beats her fists and kicks the tub like a two-year-old having a tantrum.

An hour later she makes her way downstairs. The torture continues. She is dressed like an overgrown baby in a stiff silk dress and ballet shoes, her hair held back by a ribbon. Either her grandmother is making up for lost time or she has a dark sense of humour. Bodi can see why her mother got the hell out if this was an everyday occurrence.

'Miss.' A butler standing at the foot of the stairs bows and leads her through to a huge dining room. The kind where you could sit either end of the table and shout 'pass the salt' and no one would hear you. The table isn't set and he keeps on walking so

Bodi follows him, all the while considering the layout of the house and any way she can make a run for it. She may be seen to play the game but that doesn't mean she is actually playing it. She keeps slipping in her shoes on the carpet and the underwear that had been left out for her really is for a child so she is trying with all her might not to yank it out of her bum every two steps. As much as she enjoys dressing up this is a step too far. They walk into another room. A parlour, Bodi guesses, drawing on her knowledge of the Brontës and Austen.

'How lovely! I knew there was a young lady in there somewhere under that feral street urchin.' Her tone is as condescending as a high church preacher.

Her grandmother is sat at a small table set for two. Boudicca forces a smile and sits down. She can barely see in the dim light of the candelabra. It isn't like she is short of electricity like half the city. She clearly dislikes harsh light and Bodi puts that down to vanity. She has heard that the President likes to rub the placenta of newborn babies into her skin to keep herself young. Or is it that she injects stem cells? Bodi can't quite remember. Her grandmother rings a small bell and a panel in the wall opens for a maid to bring in a huge tray. She serves them some bread and places soup in front of them. It is grey. Again, Bodi wonders if you have all the money and power in the country why would you eat grey food? So far her grandmother is unfathomable. Bodi dips her bread in her soup with her fingers and rips it off with her teeth.

'No dear. Not so rough. A nibble of bread then a sip of soup.' Her grandmother smiles but Bodi can see she is testing her very last nerve, so she carries on dipping and ripping. The soup isn't half bad. Mushroom she guesses, with a hint of something boozy. Edwina takes two sips of the soup and leaves the rest to go cold in the bowl. She sits staring at Bodi, repressing a grimace at her table manners. She rings the bell again.

Classical music fills the silence between them. Without quite finishing her mouthful Bodi attempts polite conversation.

'I know this music, I think.'

'Elgar. Perhaps your mother played it to you?' Edwina sounds pleased.

'No she's a bit more hippy singer songwriter. Perhaps it was an advert. For loo roll?'

Edwina visibly shivers at her granddaughter's vulgarity. Bodi is putting it on, she knows exactly what piece of music it is, but if Edwina wants a street urchin then she is going to get one.

The bowls are cleared and replaced with poached salmon and ribbons of vegetables. After a few hasty mouthfuls Bodi decides it is time to get the measure of her new relative.

'So Granny Edwina. What's the plan? You going to Rapunzel the hell out of Mum and me? Look us up in the tower with a spinning wheel? Feed us poisoned apples for breakfast?'

'Very literary dear, though I think you have your fairy tales muddled.'

'You get the gist,' she jibes.

'As you know, tomorrow has the potential to be a very chaotic day. I would rather leave the city altogether, but as your mother isn't quite herself we'll have to endure it from within these walls. Thomas assures me that he will have everything under control within a couple of hours so it shouldn't be too much of an inconvenience. His team are so very capable.'

'Capable is one way of looking at it. Some might say indiscriminate, brutal lapdogs to an over privileged dominatrix?'

'How awfully clever you are dear. Such wonderful words. Now I have no doubt that you've been indoctrinated from the cradle in the ways of that damned Populus but maintaining the status quo is complex, and civic order must prevail.'

'You might be surprised to hear that I didn't know Mum had been a part of Populus until about a week ago. She never spoke about it much but then again seems I didn't know about her other family either. Quite the keeper of secrets.'

'She was always like that, even as a child. Rose was a lot more straightforward though a little less spark than your mother. I always thought Ruby would follow me into politics. She always had something.'

'Well she did. Just not the brand that you were selling.'

'Quite.' Edwina cuts her dead.

'What happens now, to mum and I?' Bodi can't help feeling that yet again someone else is making decisions about her future.

'We can hardly have you gallivanting around the city causing havoc can we? As soon as we can we'll leave for my country estate. I have a small cottage there that you and your mother can live in. Away from everything. No doubt you're as enamoured with that band of miscreants as your mother but you'll soon get over that. You weren't too bothered about handing over that Balthazar cretin, were you? So maybe it won't be such a wrench. A double agent in the making...' Bodi scowls over the table though no doubt her grandmother can't see. She still has her sunglasses on after all.

'I had no choice.' Bodi doesn't know why she has to justify her actions to this monster or why she cares what her opinion is of her.

'There are always choices Boudicca. And what is right in one man's eyes is wrong in another's. As long as what you believe is right then who's to question you?'

'That mantra seems to work for you. But then again I have a conscience.'

'Possibly. Possibly not... I shall get Marie to bring your dessert to your room. As delightful as it is getting to know you I still have some state business to attend to before the morning. Do excuse me.'

'Not really,' Bodi mutters under her breath. Edwina leaves the room and Bodi sits there for a minute taking it all in. Is that it now, will they go wherever her Grandmother decrees? Has her mother moved from one prison to another?

She climbs the stairs and returns to the room where her clothes have been laid out. A single scoop of mint sorbet sits in a dish on a side table. What she wouldn't give for a sandwich! She pokes at it and tries a mouthful but leaves it to melt. Curled up against the bed headboard, she sits thinking about Reed at the gates. He must have followed her all day to find her there. He would have seen Evan hit her with her backpack and seen Balt driven off in the Sick Boys' black van. She wonders if Sam knows what Reed is up to? She hopes so, as she worries that he will do something rash and Sam is good at keeping him calm. She peers out of the window but she can't see as far as the road. She misses him already but she has to lose him to save him. Sacrificing Balt was necessary but Reed, or Evan for that matter, is so much harder.

She looks around for her backpack and finds it hidden in a wardrobe. While she has been having dinner with her grandmother all her clothes have been washed and ironed. She rummages in the pack, the details from the locket and other ruinous bits of paper are still under the lining where she had hidden them. Bodi loads her clothes back into the bag and changes into some flannel pyjamas that have been laid out for her. At least these are the right size and are plain blue, no bunnies or cartoon characters. If it wasn't for the circumstances she would have quite enjoyed the luxury of her surroundings. And the bedside table is loaded with some brilliant classics. Everything feels amazing to the touch, soft and clean. It is seductive.

The house is quiet, occasionally broken by the strangled whine of police sirens. Bodi checks the landing is clear before going through to her mother's room. Ruby is still unconscious. Her face looks a little less drawn, though Bodi realises that probably isn't possible in just a few hours. Maybe she has got used to her mum looking like this. She climbs in bed beside her mum, feeling the warmth of her body as she moves the covers. She lies her head down on the feather pillow and falls fast asleep.

'Bodi. Oh my darling girl.' A small voice wakes her from her sleep. She opens her eyes to her mother's face just inches away from hers.

'Hi Mum.' She mumbles, still drowsy. 'You okay?'

Ruby lifts her arm with the drip attached. 'Been better.' She rubs her head, still not used to her cropped hair.

'This is mental mum. Why didn't you tell me your mum was the Wicked Witch of the East?'

'West. You never got that right. The one from the East is the one the house lands on.'

'*Mum.*'

'Would you? I never thought I'd see her again, well I hoped I wouldn't. She'd already ruined my childhood I didn't need her getting her hands on yours as well.'

'I mean seriously, of all the people to be related to. And how did you escape?'

'It's a very long story. I'll bore you with it one day. Just to say she and I never really saw things the same way so I got out.' Even heavily sedated, her mum's exasperation comes through.

'I met Rose. She seems to have genuinely missed you.'

'Now that's someone I do wish had been in your life. My lovely, sweet sister. I miss her too, every day. The thought of her living with that thug! And when I saw you with him!' Ruby's faced flushes.

'Mum. What are we going to do? Edwina is talking about taking us off to the country, to some cottage in her grounds.'

'Willowbrook. I loved it there when I was a kid. It was the only time mother was nice. She's not really a city kind of person. The green seemed to calm her down a bit. We used to have lovely picnics and it always seemed to be either gloriously sunny or pelting it down.'

'Mum. Please. Concentrate.'

'Sorry, it's these drugs they're feeding me. I'm not myself. I'm sorry you've had to deal with all of this without me. I bet it's been super stressy. After all those years of being kept away from this and from Populus it must've been a massive shock. Can't help but think that you've been reliving my teenage years. Not what I wanted at all.'

Bodi sits up. 'I don't think there's time to go down the 'I wish I'd done things differently' route today Mum. I think we should leave. Like now. Before Edwina makes us disappear.'

Ruby tries to sit up but can't. She falls back on her pillow. 'Not going to happen little B. I feel dizzy even when I sit up. Tommy had me take all manner of crap when they locked me up. It's not out of my system yet. Been like a living nightmare.'

Bodi looks over at the clock which ticks loudly on the mantel-piece.

'It's 5am. If we go now then I'm sure no one will stop us,' Bodi pleads.

'You go. I'll be fine. I know how to handle mother. I'm getting quite good at hiding these pills. I'll be better in a day or two. Then we can go home. Oh, though I guess that's not there any-more. Well, Balt can find us somewhere new to live.'

'Balt's gone Mum. I had to trade him for you.'

'Oh Bodi really? But he's been so good to us.'

'It was him that shopped us. He got you taken away. He wanted me to be the new face of Populus and needed you out of the way to make that happen.'

Ruby is genuinely shocked to hear this about her old friend. 'And I sent you to him, just as he wanted. Always been too clever for his own good that one. But we're here now. If you wait with me then at least we'll be together and we can go find a new home.'

'I guess so but there's a march today mum, a huge one. It's been building for days and I think it could get really bad. And if you're still here you're a sitting duck. They're heading straight for this place and her.'

'I'm not going anywhere Bodi. I can't, look at me. You're not strong enough to carry me out of here on your own and I can't see anyone helping us. I don't trust anyone here.' Her mum starts to cry. Bodi reaches over and brushes the tears from her cheeks.

'I'm so frustrated and I feel like I'm a kid again. It's very emo-tional seeing that woman again. She's not like anyone else I've ever known in my life. I can't believe she gave birth to me!'

'You can choose your friends but not your family.' Bodi can see that this week has really taken it out of her as well. 'Maybe I can get someone to help me carry you out of here. I just need to get out first.'

'What if you get caught? Those asshole Sick Boys are every-where.'

'Well I can always say I was looking for the kitchen. What is it with rich people and food? I'm starving!'

'Is there a basement? Wherever's the furthest you can get from here I guess. I don't know this place at all, I didn't grow up here.' Ruby rubs her daughter's arm. 'You have to come back, promise me. I can't lose you again. It's been the worst week of my life.'

'Can't say it's been that much fun for me either.' Bodi smiles. 'Of course I'll come back and then we'll do a runner from the old lady.'

'I seem to have spent my life running away from her but somehow she always finds me.' Ruby sounds resigned to this situation. Bodi wants to stay to reassure her. It feels weird to leave her mum so soon after she has found her, but she has to believe that she will be safe here for a few hours.

'Right. I'm off.' She kisses her mother's cheek. 'See you in a bit Ma. Love you.'

'Love you.' Her mum lightly squeezes her hand goodbye. Bodi can feel the small amount of strength her mum has.

*M*other waved the newspaper in Ruby's face.

'What were you thinking?! THIS! I have to wake up to THIS?! I can't even…' She picked up another paper and waved it at her, and another. The image of Ruby on top of the Boudicca statue was front page news. It would seem she was now a 'hooligan', an 'anti-royalist' and a 'terrorist in the making'.

Ruby sat with her arms crossed defiantly trying to stare her mother down. Rose stared down at the kitchen table. They had been roused by their mother's hysteria and dragged from their beds.

'And you? I would have thought better of you.' She turned on Rose who stifled a sob but said nothing.

'It's not her fault. Don't shout at her,' Ruby said vehemently. 'I made her come.' Ruby didn't see any point in both of them going down for this. Rose had carried the can for her so many times before.

A sharp 'Get out!' from her mother sent Rose fleeing up the stairs, the tears now free flowing.

'I've had more than enough of you. It's time for you to pack your bags.'

'What?' Ruby was amazed. This was harsh, even for her mother.

'You heard me. Pack your bags. You so clearly don't want to be a part of this family so perhaps it's time you left.' Her mother pointed at the front door.

'You're kicking me out?!'

'I would say you've been half way out the door for some time now Ruby. I know for a fact that you haven't been going to that school I'm shelling out good money for. You come home whenever you feel like it, looking like a deranged mess. Heaven knows what drugs you're on?!'

At this Ruby rolled her eyes. She wasn't on anything. Why did adults always think you were on something if you didn't play the game? Honestly. Her mother hadn't finished: 'You treat this place like a hotel and you spend so much time with these people you might as well be one of them.'

At 'these people' Ruby rankled, she stood up to lean in to her mother.

'These people have purpose, mother. They are not just self-serving egomaniacs like some people. These people will probably have more of an impact on the country than some people ever will. These people *will tear down everything* some *people have spent their meaningless lives obsessing over.' Ruby spat the words at her mother. Relieved to have the opportunity to say what she was feeling. It felt like a weight lifted not to have to pussyfoot around her any longer.*

'Is that so? Well, good luck with that. See how you like a country that flounders without strong leadership. See how you like a country overrun by layabouts and miscreants. Every day I spend in those god-forsaken chambers...'

'You're keeping us safe. I know! But are you? Are we really safe? And what are we safe from? What's so terrible about change? What's so terrible about a little less control?'

'I am not going to stand here and have all I stand for and all I've built be torn down by my teenage daughter. You know nothing of the world. You know nothing of life. Just you wait, young lady.' Her mother was on her soapbox.

They were interrupted by the phone which her mother answered with a series of curt 'yes's'. She slammed the phone down.

'I'm being called in. I'll be hauled over the coals for this. Why, for once, could you not think of someone other than yourself?'

'That's what I was doing mother. Thinking about everyone, not just myself, not just you. God forbid you, the grand Edwina Chancellor, should get a bit of bad press. God forbid, you take my side and show me some support. And no one knows that's your daughter, not really. It's not like they've ever seen us together since we were rolled out ten years ago for photo opps. We're stuck here every day while you're off kissing arse all day and night.'

Edwina smacked her daughter in the face.

'Ungrateful little...' she muttered as Ruby stood there aghast. Her own palm comforting the spot where her mother's had struck her. Edwina left the room for the car waiting outside. 'Don't be here when I get back Ruby. And have a good life.'

MONDAY

Bodi tiptoes to her room, changes into her own clothes, and boots in hand tiptoes down the stairs. She creeps through the dining room to the parlour and pushes along the walls trying to find the hidden door the maid used at dinner. She carefully makes her way down the stairs to discover a long corridor with stone flagging and a low ceiling. Bodi can see the staff entrance at the end of the passage and an alarm panel glows next to it. She is surprised when she gets close enough to read the electronic display: "Enter code to reset alarm." Has someone forgotten to set the alarm? She thinks that is unlikely. She tries the doorknob tentatively and it swings open. The alarm doesn't go off. Seems that not everyone is loyal in the president's household.

Shutting the door quietly behind her, she crouches down behind a low garden wall to work out what her next move might be. The sodden thud of the weary patrolman's boots march by her head. Once he is safely round the corner she creeps low and slow to the back of the garden and hides behind a bush. Barbed wire covers the top of the wall, there is no way she can get over that. She feels around the wall, clambering over flower beds and trying to disappear into the shadows. She finds a recess. Trailing ivy covers a small wooden gate with a bolt across. Good for keeping people out but not ideal for keeping them in. She scrapes the bolt across bit by bit trying not to make a sound and carefully opens the gate. She had found a tiny hand mirror on the dressing table in her room, she pokes it out into the street to see what she is up against. 'Reading old crime novels really comes in handy sometimes,' she thinks. A guard is propped up right next to the gate. His rifle's barrel rests against his leg, the butt on the floor. His hat has fallen over his face, resting on his nose, and a small snore emanates from under it. 'Tut, tut, sleeping on the job,' Bodi reprimands. She prays that the door has been oiled recently but no such luck. Every single time she edges it an inch it groans louder. There is nothing else for it, she has to give it one huge push and run. She kicks the gate with all her might and it swings back and hits the guard full on.

'Stop!' the startled guard shouts after her, fumbling for his gun. 'Stop right there!' By the time he has got the rifle in position she is round the corner and on her way. Someone is watching over her today, she is sure of it. Making use of the abandoned streets, she races through the no man's land. Her greatest fear is that riots would lead to yet more oppression. They all have to find a way to manage the march so that real change can begin, rather than them being written off as imbeciles and arsonists.

Walking through more residential areas, she notices that people are up much earlier than usual. Smoke curls from chimneys and small shafts of light escape from drawn curtains. Neighbours are moving between houses, carrying sleeping children, food and flasks. It is like watching a silent black and white movie. Bodi notices that every single adult she sees is dressed like her, head to toe in black. This is no ordinary day of rest. There is a noticeable hum of anticipation as they prepare to protest. Populus is no longer the driving force behind the march. The people are also rising up to reclaim their city.

Bodi walks up to the top of Primrose Hill. Groups of people are already gathering there, eyes squinting against the sunrise that heralds the start of this extraordinary Halloween day. Most have painted their faces or have homemade masks perched on top of their heads. Word has got round that TrueSec will be recording their every movement and as brave as they are, people want to hide their identities. The mood is convivial though that belies an underlying current of nerves and tension. They are walking into the unknown and are scared that what is intended to be a peaceful protest will inevitably turn ugly. Despite their anger and hunger for change, they aren't violent people. They have lived through enough of that already. They want to rebuild their lives. Be heard.

Bodi spots Sam and makes her way over to him.

'You managed to follow them from the meet yesterday?' she says, skipping any formal hellos.

'Yes, we know where they're holding him. We've had someone on it all night and we have a few contacts working inside so if he's moved we'll know about that as soon as it happens.'

'And Reed?'

'I persuaded him to lead another group coming in from south London.' Sam says.

'Good. Best he's kept out of it.'

Sam nods. A hunting horn bellows behind them.

'Sounds like it's time to go,' Bodi says, a frisson of excitement in her voice.

Sam hands her a mask. It is white with blue war paint smeared across both eyes.

'I thought it was about time our new warrior queen came out to play,' Sam says theatrically.

Her breath flushes across her face behind the mask. It is claustrophobic but also reassuring. No one, friend or foe, will recognise her with it on. The group starts walking down the hill in silence. The closer they get to the centre of the city more and more people join them. Leaving their homes and loved ones behind them, men and women in black with painted faces or masks come out of houses and snake in behind them. Their numbers swell at every junction. They are a silent, black river of skulls flowing into the heart of the city.

Nerves start to jangle as they encounter groups of Sick Boys. No one marching looks at or acknowledges them. The march continues in silence through the streets. Ultimately they want rid of these jumped up militia but that is not their fight today, their sights are set on bigger things. The traffic has stopped, doors shut, shops shuttered. The city has responded to its people's wishes and left the veins free for the blood to flow to its heart, to give it new life. Bodi walks near the front of her group alongside

Sam. Masks hide the faces of the other Populus members but she knows they are each leading a group that joins them along the way. They walk down Park Lane where the once luxurious hotels are run like mini citadels. Places of gambling and trafficking, where people fight for their lives every single day. Gangs and slumlords rule the streets here, a reimagining of Fagin's London. There are hollers from the windows and wolf whistles as they pass but most of the residents are too strung out to take in what is happening outside.

By now the march is tens of thousands strong. Progress is getting slower as they meet more and more groups at Wellington Arch. The Sick Boys have set up a huge roadblock there and the march halts. Guns are loaded but pointed skyward. Even TrueSec acknowledge that this is a riot in the making, and so much bigger than anything they have seen before.

A voice bellows from a tannoy system: 'Return to your homes. This is an unlawful demonstration. You can go no further.'

The crowd stand firm. They are not going to fall at the first hurdle. Still no one speaks. This tactic unnerves the guards, they are used to verbal abuse giving them reason to retaliate. They repeat the warning. By now they are surrounded and outnumbered. Sam rifles through some sheets of paper, looks up and studies the faces to determine who is who among the guards. He steps forward and proffers one of the pieces of paper to a grunt who takes it and passes it to the superior Sam has been eyeballing. He balks, looks around him and commands: 'Stand down. Let them through.' The guards look surprised. His deputy questions him but he isn't going to change his mind. They move the barriers back slowly.

'What is on that piece of paper?' Bodi whispers to Sam when he resumes his place next to her.

'His home address. The address of his mother. His sister's and his in-laws. Even the big dogs won't bite when their families are involved,' Sam says.

Bodi doesn't need to ask how he has got the information. Balt has been working on this plan for years, and his plan is being seen through to the letter even if he isn't there to execute it.

'Do you have people there? Holding them?' Bodi doesn't really want to know the answer.

'Maybe. Maybe not. But he has no way of finding that out right now. The power of information trumps brute force once again, my dear.'

They start to lead the rally forward again. The sheer number of people joining the protest makes for very slow going. As they make their way through Green Park, Bodi looks towards the walls of Clarence House. Her mum is still in there most probably facing questions about her daughter's whereabouts. She promised Ruby she would be back in a couple of hours, though she hadn't said she would be returning with tens of thousands of people. While this is still a peaceful demonstration Bodi fears for her mum's safety. If this turns bad Clarence House will be one of the first places to get ransacked. She tries to move towards the gates but she can't get across the crowd. They are packed in and there is no way to change course. Sam grabs her hand and pulls her back towards him.

'Don't get lost. We need to stick together,' he hisses at her.

'Did you know, about who my grandmother was?' she asks.

'I had my suspicions. Now shhh.'

They get to Old Parliament Square eventually. Bodi sees a truck loaded with speakers is leading their sister march across Westminster Bridge from the south. She can see a familiar figure standing at the front of the truck. The face paint and clothes cannot conceal Reed from her. He grips the side of the truck's cab and looks like he has shed the boy she had first met.

She has to get to him. He will help her get Ruby away from Edwina. But she knows that if she runs to him things will start to fall apart. The crowd will follow her lead and there could be casualties. She moves carefully across the front of her group leaving Sam looking round for her. She skirts round the edges, aware that the Sick Boys are watching everything, weapons in hand. She doesn't fancy a baton to the kidneys so walks with the group a little further. When a gap appears, she tries to run across to meet Reed's truck but before she can get there an arm reaches out and grabs her.

'What the...! Get off me!' she yelps.

'Shhh!' Her assailant lifts his mask. Evan slams her back against the wall next to him. She wriggles her arm from his grip, trying to summon the self-defence techniques that Balt had taught her. She's sure neither of them anticipated she would be using them on Evan.

'Evan, what are you doing? How did you even know it was me?' He lifts a stray red curl that has escaped out of the side of her hoodie. She tucks it back in.

'I have to get to Reed. I need his help with something,' she begs.

'No way Boo. You're coming with me. I don't know what you've cooked up with Sam but I can't see my dad anywhere about, can you? This is his march and he's not here to lead it. It's not right. You and me, we need to go see your old mate Tommy the Sick Boy and get him back.'

'Not now Ev. It's all in hand. Honestly.' She lifts her mask and looks at him. She sees in his eyes the sadness and fear that she has felt for the past week.

'How can I trust you now?' his voice breaks, despite his bluster. He feels she has betrayed him and she feels terrible because it is true.

'I'm so sorry Ev. Really.' She squeezes his hand. He slumps against the wall.

'Promise me we'll get him back. Can you promise?' his eyes plead with her. He looks like a young child.

How can I promise anything right now? she thinks. There's no way I want Balt leading anything after what he did to me and mum, but I don't want him to die and I definitely don't want to lose Evan. She leans in and gives him a hug.

'It's on you,' he whispers in her ear.

'Feels like everything is right now,' she says.

Bodi takes advantage of Evan being off guard to run to Reed's truck. He pulls her up by one hand.

'It's not safe for you here B. You need to go. If anyone finds out...'

he stops. He looks towards the road that leads to the President's residence.

'Who I am? Reed, *I* didn't even know that until yesterday. How can I be responsible for that?!' she says.

'It won't matter to them. The truth tends to go unnoticed at times like these,' he replies.

'I need your help. My mum, she's being held hostage in there and I can't get her out by myself. They've drugged her and she's too weak to escape.'

'How? Tell me. How can we do that Bodi?'

'Just come. Please.'

Someone pulls at her leg and Bodi grabs hold of Reed. It is Evan. She kicks back, clinging onto Reed but it is no good, the three of them land in a heap at the side of the truck.

Reed leaps at Evan, fists flying. 'Don't touch her!' he yells. The Sick Boys notice and are on their way over, happy to have someone to get stuck into.

'Guys. Stop! We're getting all the wrong kind of attention. This is just what they want so they can start laying in to everyone,' Bodi says tersely.

She works her way between the two of them, snatches both their hands and scrambles through to the other side of the truck.

'If you touch her again,' Reed spits his fury at Evan.

'What?! What will you do? As if!' Evan replies.

'Seriously. Stop!' Bodi hisses.

The Square is full and people are standing in silence. Suddenly Balt's voice booms from the speakers at the back of the truck.

'London, you have come in your thousands, your tens of thousands, to take your city back!' The crowd cheer and it is deafening after so much silence.

'What the hell?!' Bodi and Evan are confused, looking round for Balt.

'It's a recording.' Reed points at the cab of the truck where Fergus is sitting.

The grainy sound fills the air above the square. People strain to hear what is being said through the crude sound system. A generator whirs on the truck and occasionally it stops and judders.

'This is your home and your life but it is not your own, it no longer belongs to you. For too many years we have suffered at the hands of the President and her militia.' The crowd boo, willing participants in the theatrics of the event. The recording continues: 'Most of us remember a time when we had a say in how we lived. When we lived in freedom and prospered. When we could drink and dance in the evenings with our loved ones and chat with our neighbours on the streets without fear of being arrested. When we could look forward to a bright future for our children. When we could buy the food we needed to live, enjoy the money we worked for.'

Bodi looks around. Lots of people are nodding and grumbling their agreement. 'We can have that again. It can be ours, again. It is time that every man and woman of London stands up and says 'yes'! Say it with me: 'Yes!'. We want a new life. YES. We want our communities to thrive. YES. We want to be free of brutality. YES. We want to earn a decent living. YES. We want education for everyone. YES. We want healthcare for everyone. YES. We want the power to run our own lives.'

Cheers and resounding echoes of 'yes' ripple through the crowd. He is like an evangelist preacher whipping up the crowd into euphoria. As much as he thinks he has everyone's good intentions at heart, he still has to be the leader that gets them there.

'We are not children. We are smart people. We can make our own decisions. And I urge you, I implore you, to take that step today. To take that first step towards a new city. Reclaim your city London. Reclaim the power! It's time to take action.'

Bodi can feel the energy off the crowd. Balt will be able to get these people to do anything he wants now.

'Turn to the authorities. Face them and say NO.' The crown turns towards the Sick Boys standing guard around them. 'Take the city back London. Make it your own again. Will we stand for this? No. Do you control us? No. Are we going to take this anymore? No.'

'No! No! No!' rings out around them. The crowd is starting to turn. Men link arms. Women scream in the faces of the police. Fence posts and hoardings are being torn down to create make-shift weapons.

Bodi looks at Reed. 'We have to do something. He's kicking off the riot. People are going to get hurt,' she says. Before he can reply she runs off. She can hear Reed and Evan shouting her name behind her but she has her mind set on it.

Surging bodies force her to swim upstream. It takes all her effort to reach the cab and when she gets there the door is locked. She bangs on the window and Fergus reaches over and winds down the window.

'Boudicca, you can't be here!' he shouts. She pushes the window down and climbs into the cab. Her legs sticking out of the window, she pushes the power button on the car radio. Balt's voice disappears. A few people still chant in the background but it dies down as the crowd turn back to the truck to see what is going on. Bodi ejects the CD and Fergus tries to grab it but she scrambles out of the cab before he can reach her. She stands on the back of the truck poised to jump off and get away but all eyes are on her. They are expecting something from her. She tries to get down but there is nowhere to go, people start to jostle the truck. She clings on as they vent their frustration at her for ending the show. Making a split decision she climbs up the speakers and stands on top of them. She whips off her mask and her hood. She is not going to be a faceless voice inciting violence. She starts to shout but realises no one can hear her. Looking around she spots Reed and he's handing her a microphone.

'My name is Boudicca Jones and I love London.' A tentative cheer rises near her. Bodi wracks her brains for what to say. 'But I'm coming to realise that London no longer loves us. She is not what she was. She is tired and fragile, and frankly, she is over us. She wants us to move on and leave her in peace to die with dignity. She has stood here for a few thousand years and everything we have done in recent memory, whether it's for the 'good of the people' or more often the good of a few, has dragged her backwards. We cling onto the idea of her as a great city, as the heart of all things, but she's not. We have ruined her, trampled on her and we are all to blame. We stopped caring. We stopped noticing.

'We used to be great. We stood up for what was right. Had a code we lived by. Fought against poverty, not poor people. You know what, we *saw* people. Saw each other.' Bodi takes a deep breath. She is gradually winning people over. The crowd is quieter, straining to hear what she says.

'I know that you love London too and that you want to build her back up again. You came here today because you want every street to be safe and you want to be happy to go to work in the morning. You want the perpetual misery of Edwina Chancellor's presidency to end, today. But is more fighting the answer? Is more violence the answer?'

Someone heckles her from the crowd: 'Go home little girl!'

Bodi laughs.

'I would love to go home! I *wish* I could go home. And I know I look like a little girl to you but I am a young woman. I've had to grow up very quickly; learn how to take care of myself, in this society that keeps taking and gives little in return. This week I have lived both sides of this sad story. The authorities took my mum away, but it was the people she trusted the most that gave her up.' Bodi stops, holding back tears when she thinks of Ruby.

'It's trust that we don't have anymore. Trust in the people that govern us. Trust in those that want to change things. Trust in what we truly believe is right. Most importantly we no longer have trust in each other.'

The crowd is calming down. People are listening to her. Bodi's stops and tries to take a deep breath. Reed, who is crouched on the bed of the truck, smiles at her, encouraging her to continue.

'The people holding those guns, yes, those ones right next to you, are Londoners too. They are doing a job, just like you do, to support their families. I have been afraid of these men my entire life. I have *hated* them my entire life. I didn't see them as people. But I do now. I ask you, I implore you, to please see us as people as well.'

The Sick Boys stand firm. Bodi had hoped they would retreat a little. Show some signs of understanding. Maybe that was a stretch? she thinks. Undeterred, Bodi turns back to the crowd. All eyes are on her.

'Do you want to destroy even more of our city? Do you want to burn more of it to the ground and turn it into an even worse place to live? Do you think our voices will be heard if the rest of the city hate us? If we aren't seen as people but as thugs and arsonists?

'Think of the consequences. There are other ways for us to be heard. Reasonable and right ways to redeem the city. Ways that don't destroy our homes. Ways to rebuild our lives here, where everyone is heard. We can-' The microphone is grabbed roughly from her hand. She feels a strong arm wrap round her shoulder, fingers tight round her bicep. It is Balt, standing on the roof of the cabin. 'How has he got out so quickly?' she panics. The deal was that he would be let go only once the march was over.

'Let's have a cheer for our young friend here.' Balt roars. The crowd cheers in response. His outer persona oozes control, but closer up Bodi can see his eyes are seething with rage. She is ruining his big day. She pushes the microphone down and it reverbs.

'You can't be here Balt. They want you dead.'

And almost as if Bodi commanded it, an order is declared and the guards around the perimeter pick up their guns and aim them at Balt. The crowd scream and rush towards the truck. People are getting trampled. Balt uses the cover of the chaos to jump down from the cab and drags Bodi with him. He pushes her down towards Reed with a forced smile.

'You gotta break a few eggs to make an omelette!' he says, delighted. He is clearly getting a huge buzz from the bedlam happening around them. 'Go! You've done your bit. Fly home to mummy, little bird.' He jumps off the back of the truck and runs away from them, grabbing Evan by the arm and pulls him along with him. A barrage of gunfire pummels the air.

Petrified, Reed and Bodi clamber off the truck. Bodi can't be-

lieve that she was minutes away from turning things around
and yet again Balt swooped in to ruin things. They run towards
her grandmother's residence, through the streets which are a
riot of beatings and screaming. Their ears still ringing, they hear
more gunfire resounding around the Square. Balt couldn't have
orchestrated it better.

At Green Park they find people pushing at the gates of Clarence
House; some to escape the crush, others to tear it down along
with the people inside it. Lit petrol bombs are pitched over the
gates aimed at dispersing the guards. Reed follows Bodi as she
runs down a side road. She is going to the gate she had left by this
morning. People are following them, thinking that she is going
to ransack the house. The guard at that gate is now two guards,
both with their rifles cocked. Bodi approaches them calmly and
holds her hands up to stop the crowd behind her from following.

'Please. I'd like to go in. My mother is inside. She is Edwina Chancellor's daughter, Ruby,' she says. The crowd mutter at this rev-
elation. 'If you could just radio through, they will tell you that's
the case. I need to see her.'

The guards laugh in her face.

'The little revolutionary is the president's granddaughter. Do
me a favour. I know you see us as 'people' now and that's all very
nice, young lady, but I can't let you in. I'm not feeling like much
of a people person right now.' More laughter.

'Thomas Cleaver is my uncle. Your boss. I'm sure he'd like to
hear about how unhelpful you've been.' She thinks it's worth
a try but the guards look at each other nonplussed. Her uncle
opens the gate behind them. 'How does he always know...?' she
marvels.

'Bit late to play the little princess card isn't it Boudicca? 'Don't
you know who I am?'' he whines. 'Unfortunately for you, I do.
And it's way too late. They've gone Boudicca. You don't think
the grand madame would hang around for your sorry soliloquy,
do you? She left as soon those ugly, old boots of yours hit the
pavement. And as for mommy dearest, she's right by her side,

drugged up to the eyeballs. Right boys, grab her!'
Two of the guards put down their guns to go for Bodi but the crowd take their opportunity to rush the gate. Reed grabs Bodi and pulls her to the floor, covering her with his body as the crowds trample over them to get inside. The people lunge at Thomas and he disappears under the barrage of a dozen boots. Reed rolls Bodi to one side she starts to scream. Reed yelps, holding onto his side where he has been crushed.

'I said I'd come back for her. I said it would be okay. And now she's gone.' Sobs wrack Bodi's whole body. She is a million miles away from the euphoria she felt when she addressed the crowd. 'And Sam, where's Sam?' She is panicky.

'He'll be fine B. He has a way of keeping out of trouble. Probably found the only pub that's open and holed up there.' A tremor in Reed's voice shows that though he is joking he is worried too. Sam is all the family he has in the world. 'We've got to get out of here. Get home. It's all kicking off. The Sick Boys are just itching to annihilate the lot of us. I'm not sure that 'we're all people' thing quite did the job!' Even though he is mocking her Bodi laughs. She punches him in the arm.

'I didn't have much time to work on it,' she laments.

They look up and down the street. Some people are still trying to leave but others are fighting. Makeshift petrol bombs are being handed along to the front line. The Sick Boys are moving in en masse towards the heart of the action and there are only a few minutes before they are trapped here.

'Where's Evan?' Bodi feels responsible for him. Her fight and his are bound together now and though Balt is free she still needs to make things right with him.

'I don't know B but we've got to go *now*. If we leave it any longer we'll get kettled in and we'll all get burned alive. Let's go. Now!'

They keep to the edge of the wall and Bodi pulls her hood up so that she won't be recognised. Trails of red run like veins through the debris of discarded masks and banners, draining the streets of their earlier energy, and the air is thick with the smell of smoke, blood and vomit. The sound of smashing glass, the shattering whoosh of the petrol coming alight, the screams of the protestors and the steady bang of the Sick Boys' batons against riot shields is their new soundtrack. The reality of the riot is much more terrifying than anyone could have imagined.

Bodi runs but her legs feel separate from her body. Her head is back in that room at the Residence, her mum lying next to her and Bodi promising to return. She can never take that decision back. She chose to leave and now she will be as hunted as one of faces of Populus. She is officially one of them and unless the riots are successful – and how do you measure that kind of success? – she has lost all her freedom. Reed pulls her into a side street and flattens her against the wall with his body. He starts kissing her.

'Now? We're doing this now?' she manages to get out before he kisses her again. Out of the corner of her eye she spots a large group of TrueSec guards marching past. A couple of them nudge each other and one of them makes the peace sign with his fingers.

'Make love not war, man.'

Bodi looks away from them and pretends to be a teenage girl whose only concern is kissing her boyfriend. 'If only that were the case,' she thinks.

As they pass through the streets they see that the fighting is not confined to the centre of the city. Being at the front of the march neither of them had realised the volume of people marching. And though some have run home to escape trouble, many are still brawling. Some people are trying to leave but they are cordoned off by row upon row of Sick Boys.

'We should help them,' Bodi says, struggling to leave people behind.

'Yes we should B but we can't. The minute the guards work out who you are they'll make an example of you. I'm not going to let that happen,' he says, trying to be kind but sounding irritated.

It is getting increasingly more difficult to get along the roads. Either because of serious walls of fire, or because the demonstrators or the Sick Boys are blocking streets.

'I don't think we'll make home, or to St James's,' Reed says, he is exhausted and panting. He rubs his eyes which are streaming with tears, he holds his side which is bleeding. Smoke fills the streets and makes moving anywhere hard going. Bodi looks around. She sees somewhere familiar. It is the last place she wants to go but they have little choice. She points up above them a couple of streets over.

'What's that then?' he asks.

'Balt's flat.'

'You are insane. Certifiably insane.' he drags himself along behind her.

When they get to the foot of the stairs they are met by a huge pile of furniture. The residents have thrown all they can down the stairwell to create a barricade to prevent the Sick Boys from getting in. Reed and Bodi pull some things out of the way and endeavour to climb over the pile of old sofas and sideboards.

'Maybe we should rethink this, cos there's still more than a dozen floors to walk up afterwards!' Bodi is laughing, slightly hysterically.

'At least there'll be a good view,' he jokes.

The two of them have picked a weird time to see the funny side of things. They laugh until their sides ache, Reed gripping his ribs. 'Ow. Shut up B. God! Enough!'

She pulls him over the final piece of furniture and they begin the long climb up to Balt and Evan's flat. Half way up they stop for a breather.

'How did Balt get free anyway?' Reed asks Bodi.

'I'm not very proud of it. But if you can't beat them join them...' she hesitates, she doesn't want Reed to see this side of her.

'What did you do this time?!' he asks.

'While I kept Thomas busy with Evan and Balt; Morag, Flip and some others went to Thomas's house. They held Rose until Edwina instructed Thomas let Balt go.'

'That's harsh B.'

'I know. I do. It's hideous. I don't even want to think about it. Doing that to poor Rose, but we had no choice. Tit for tat. That's what it comes down to at times like this. My mum is going to freak when she finds out. If she ever finds out. If I ever see her again...But Rose is fine. Well I hope she is. I have no idea.'

'Even after everything you want it all to be okay, don't you? That's pretty amazing.'

'Really? I think it's cowardly but I'm not sure there was much else I could do. As much as I don't want Balt in my life I couldn't take away Evan's only parent.'

They get to the top floor puffing and panting. Bent double they see a skewed view of their city through a broken window in the stairwell. Just like before, at a distance, the city skyline stands as it has stood for many years. Its vast majesty seems untouched.

'That one,' she says, pointing at Balt's front door just as it opens. The sound of something mechanical whirring fills the hallway. Evan bounds out with a cardboard box in his hands and stops still when he sees them.

'Er, alright?' he greets them as if they've just met outside the corner shop.

Reed raises his head and grunts. 'Ev.'

Bodi looks between them, confused. Boys' behaviour is still so alien to her. Only minutes ago they had been laying into each other.

'Nice speech Boo. Really got me here.' Evan sniggers and pounds his chest. Reed quietly joins in the laughter.

'It's like dealing with children. Honestly, little children,' she says and storms into the flat leaving them outside.

Balt's 'war room' is trashed. The sound she had heard outside is an old printer churning out pages steadily in the corner. Bodi wades through the ripped maps and piles of papers to see what is being printed. She picks up the pale yellow paper to read:

"NO to Chancellor. President's granddaughter leads the fight."

Above the text is a grainy black and white image of Bodi standing on the top of the sound system. It is almost a replica of the image of her mum on the Boudicca monument.

Bodi stares out of the window considering the impact of this one piece of paper. The boys both come in behind her.

'What's happened here? Did someone break in?' Reed asks Evan.

'Nah. Dad wanted it to look like that so the Sick Boys wouldn't find all his research. He sent me back to get rid of loads of stuff. It'd do damage in the wrong hands,' Evan says.

He lifts the box to indicate that's what is inside. Some of the yellow photocopies fall off the top and flutter to the floor. Reed bends down to pick one up. His jaw drops.

'What the hell…?' Reed says.

Bodi turns to them, her eyes sadly accepting the inevitability of it. 'It's what Balt wanted all along. And I walked right into it. A new face for his new revolution.'

'But you obviously really believe in it or you wouldn't have fronted out the crowd like you did,' Evan says.

'But this.' She sweeps her arm across the view where the streets are on fire and people are hurt if not dying. 'Who wants to be the face of this?'

'It's just change Boo. It's all happening for a reason.' Evan recites his father's doctrine, not altogether convincingly.

Reed baits Evan. 'Ev, you've got to get your own thoughts mate. You've seen what's going on down there. It's not exactly a birthday party, is it?'

Leaving them debating the situation, Bodi opens the door out onto the balcony. The flyers follow her out on a gust of wind, some floating down to the street below. Has she ever been in a position to stop the violence? She thinks that she has been in control of her own life because she was off the grid, but she wasn't, her mum wasn't. Who is free? Who can say genuinely that they hold their destiny in their own hands?

Reed and Evan join her on the balcony and look around them as the city they love is engulfed in flames. Not one of them knows where their parents or guardians are, or if they are even alive. Each of the boys takes one of Bodi's hands. From now on they have to forge their own futures.

＊ ＊ ＊

Acknowledgements

Thanks to my wonderful parents John and Vivien who have shown me that women can and must achieve great things. And to my family for always being hilarious and outrageous and kind.

Thanks to The Birds, Malcolm, Jack and Andrew for their help with this project and insistence that I persevere.

Thanks to Anne Heasell for her glorious cover design.

And, if I may be so bold, to London, for always stepping up and surviving everything that is thrown at it.

ABOUT THE AUTHOR

Rebecca Ward

Rebecca lives in London where she has worked in fashion and the arts for the past 25 years. As well as writing, she enjoys singing, performing as part of an amateur drama company and designing and making costumes.

Rebecca has an MA in English and Contemporary Cultural Theory from Goldsmiths.

Printed in Poland
by Amazon Fulfillment
Poland Sp. z o.o., Wrocław

60507396R00113